C000193596

Kym Rutherford returns to nurse at St Alphage's
after seven years' absence to find that the old hospital
has been replaced by a gleaming modern building.
But nothing can demolish her memories . . .

Books you will enjoy
in our Doctor–Nurse series

NURSE OVERBOARD by Meg Wisgate
EMERGENCY NURSE by Grace Read
DOCTORS IN DISPUTE by Jean Evans
WRONG DOCTOR JOHN by Kate Starr
AUSTRIAN INTERLUDE by Lee Stafford
SECOND CHANCE AT LOVE by Zara Holman
TRIO OF DOCTORS by Lindsay Hicks
CASSANDRA BY CHANCE by Betty Neels
SURGEON IN DANGER by Kate Ashton
VENETIAN DOCTOR by Elspeth O'Brien
IN THE NAME OF LOVE by Hazel Fisher
DEAR DOCTOR MARCUS by Barbara Perkins
RAINBOW SUMMER by Sarah Franklin
SOLO SURGEON by Lynne Collins
NEW DOCTOR AT THE BORONIA by Lilian Darcy
HEALERS OF THE NIGHT by Anne Vinton
THE RETURN OF DR BORIS by Lisa Cooper
DOCTOR IN NEW GUINEA by Dana James
PARIS NURSE by Margaret Barker
ROSES FOR CHRISTMAS by Betty Neels
NURSE IN BERMUDA by Helen Upshall
NURSE BRYONY by Rhona Trezise
THE FAITHFUL FAILURE by Kate Norway

YESTERDAY'S LOVE

BY

JUDITH WORTHY

MILLS & BOON LIMITED
London · Sydney · Toronto

First published in Great Britain 1984
by Mills & Boon Limited, 15–16 Brook's Mews,
London W1A 1DR

ISBN 0 263 74543 0

Set in 10 on 11 pt Linotron Times
03/0184

Photoset by Rowland Phototypesetting Ltd
Bury St Edmunds, Suffolk
Made and printed in Great Britain by
Richard Clay (The Chaucer Press) Lta
Bungay, Suffolk

CHAPTER ONE

ON HER first morning back at St Alphage's General Hospital, Nurse Kym Rutherford felt very strange, as well as apprehensive. There was nothing familiar about the ward, men's medical, except its name, Wren. When the old yellow-brick, grimy Victorian buildings had been pulled down to make way for the spanking new complex of steel and concrete, London's newest and most modern hospital, she had been far away in Australia and had not even known about it.

The first time she had walked across the sweep of concrete paving that replaced the old cobbled forecourt, she had felt a pang of regret, and some disappointment. Only the old ornate iron gates and their supporting brick pillars, topped with huge iron lamps, remained as a monument to the nineteenth-century building which had stood on the site. The new hospital had also kept the names of the main wards—Wren, Johnson, Pepys; Mildred, Katherine, Anne; and others with a flavour of the historic City.

Kym had done her training at the old St Alphage's. They might have demolished the old buildings but nothing could demolish her memories, and this morning they were flooding back unchecked, bringing with them a fresh surge of apprehension. This morning she would have to face *him*.

She had tried to picture his face and imagine his reactions, almost as often as she had rehearsed her own words and the cool, calm, matter-of-fact way she intended to deliver them: 'Harley . . . could I speak to you privately sometime? I have something important to tell you.' And every time her heart pounded in her chest like a sledgehammer, and she doubted she had the courage to go through with it.

'Nurse . . . !'

The slight impatience in Sister Muir's voice snapped Kym out of her reverie and made her realise that Sister must have summoned her before and she had not heard. Day-dreaming on her first morning on the ward was hardly the way to start! She hastily closed the linen cupboard door, and marked off the inventory sheet.

'Yes, sorry, coming . . .' she faltered like a first-year student, but she need not have worried. Sister Muir was a gentle authoritarian who achieved efficiency and co-operation from her nurses without often raising her voice. She was aware of Kym's situation, that she had been away from nursing for some years, and she was prepared to make allowances—at the start anyway.

'I want you to set up the examination trolley,' she told Kym. 'Dr Garfield is very particular and he'll throw a fit if there's so much as a square of gauze missing or out of place.'

His name! *Dr Garfield.* It plunged like a scalpel into her heart and the blade twisted as she realised how imminent her encounter now was. A vacuum seemed to have formed in her stomach and there was an uncomfortable pressing sensation behind her eyes. The urge to run headlong out of the ward was strong, but she forced herself to remember that it was for Simon's sake she was there, and gritted her teeth.

'I'll do it right away,' she said in a small, rather breathless voice, that made Sister look at her sideways and say:

'You're nervous, aren't you?'

Kym nodded, with a brief apologetic smile. Sister Muir of course had no idea just how nervous she was, or why. She thought it was only because Kym had returned to nursing after seven years away from it.

She patted Kym's arm understandingly. 'There's no

need to be. I was away from nursing for over ten years while my children were small, and I thought I'd never be able to take up where I'd left off, but I did.'

Kym was grateful for the encouragement, but she said doubtfully, 'I expect you were much more experienced, though. I'd only just qualified.'

Sister Muir nodded. 'True. But I'm sure you'll be into the swing of things in no time.' She regarded Kym sympathetically. 'It was very tragic for you to be left alone so young, and with a baby, too. The DNO told me.'

Kym averted her eyes. She could feel her cheeks turning pink. It had seemed so easy in Australia being Mrs Rutherford, but back here she flinched whenever anyone sympathised with her widowhood because it wasn't true.

After a slight pause, Sister Muir made an effort to brighten the conversation again. 'I'm quite sure an attractive lass like you will get married again one of these days.' She laughed. 'There are plenty of eligible young doctors around here for a start. Take Dr Garfield for instance . . . well, he's not as young as some of them of course, and he doesn't seem to have marriage on his mind, but he is the hospital heart-throb, and always has been, I gather. I really don't know how he's managed to stay single.' She chuckled, then asked, 'Was he here in your time?'

'Oh—yes, he was,' Kym managed to say. 'He . . . he was just a houseman then, if I recall.' She hoped she had given the impression that she scarcely knew the man. Another lie! She recalled only too well. Every single detail . . .

'Well, there's work to be done,' said Sister Muir briskly, 'and we'd better get on with it. If you'll just see to the trolley . . .'

She bustled off and Kym was thankful to have ended their conversation. Sister Muir was trying to be very understanding, but it only served to bring back the past more vividly than ever, and heighten her apprehension.

At first Kym had known a fleeting surge of joy when she had discovered she was going to have Harley Garfield's child, but it had faded instantly, to be followed by dismay and despair. Her next frantic thought had been that she must get rid of it, but that too was quickly followed by a revulsion so great she knew she could not do it. If only, she kept thinking miserably, they had stayed with the casual carefree and uncomplicated relationship they had enjoyed for several months before the Nurses' Ball.

Harley had partnered her at the ball and it had been a sparkling evening. There had been a few hi-jinks amongst the more ebullient members of staff, and by the end of the evening most people were a bit merry. Somebody had dared Harley to spend the night in the nurses' home, and Kym had let herself be persuaded to smuggle him in. It was meant to be a harmless prank, with donations from everybody to the hospital fund as their reward for not being caught.

They almost had been caught by the home's very strict supervisor, and on reaching Kym's room, flushed with success, they had dissolved into a bout of uncontrollable but stifled giggling. When it subsided they were left with an odd feeling of anti-climax. They had stood for a few moments, transfixed, as though seeing each other for the first time, and then, as though impelled by some unseen force, had fallen into each other's arms, plunged head-long into a storm of passion neither of them could control.

When dawn broke, and they disentangled themselves from each other's arms, there had been a moment of exquisite tenderness while the aura of the night still clung to them, before realisation sank in, and they drew apart, suddenly startled by what had happened. They had looked at each other, slightly appalled, each apologising to the other, both somehow embarrassed. They had talked for a while, with Harley telling Kym his plans for the future with a new heightened emphasis. They had talked like this before, but that morning she had known he was regretting, not their lovemaking, but his rash words of love during the night, and was afraid she might read more into it than he had intended. Kym had reassured him that she had no intention of settling down for a long while herself, that she wanted to make a career of nursing first, and travel as much as she could.

It was only later, after she had smuggled him out again, that Kym had realised the reason for the terrible heaviness that seemed to have descended on her. She was in love with Harley. Unknowingly she had been falling in love with him for some time, perhaps even subconsciously denying it because she knew she would only get hurt. But the previous night her feelings had overwhelmed her, and she had let him make love to her regardless of the consequences.

Sadly, she made a decision. She knew Harley would never be serious about her, but he might want to continue their relationship in its new phase, a purely physical affair. Although her body ached for him, she knew that kind of involvement would never be enough for her. Her love was new enough, she believed, to be easily quashed, so as she did not want to risk being hurt any more than she was already, when he asked her out a day or two later, she refused. He was naturally a bit surprised, even annoyed when she rejected him several more times, and finally asked coolly if the relationship was over. Steeling herself, she had said yes.

Trying hard to get over it quickly, she had gone out with other men, pretending to have a good time; but she kept noticing that Harley was never short of female companionship, and the jealousy she felt whenever she saw him with another girl told her that her feelings had not altered, and that depressed her.

Her misery, however, was not complete, until the day she finally acknowledged what she had desperately been trying not to believe, that she was pregnant. Once or twice she had made up her mind to tell Harley, so great was her need for him at that time, but always she decided against it. She would never force a man to marry her, she vowed. What kind of marriage would that be? She would probably lose him in the end anyway. So, after many sleepless nights of soul-searching, she decided to leave St Alphage's.

The next hurdle was telling her mother why, but in the event, breaking the news was less traumatic than Kym feared. Irene Andrews was shocked, but sympathetic. She could not understand why Kym refused to tell the baby's father, but she accepted in the end that she had good reasons. Kym did not even tell her who it was. She intended that to remain her secret forever.

It was Irene's idea to go to Australia and make a new life. She had cousins there and they seemed happy enough. It was also her idea that Kym become Mrs Rutherford, taking her own maiden name and pretending to be a widow. Kym would rather have stuck to the truth, that she was an unmarried mother, since few people pointed the finger nowadays, but her mother was a bit old-fashioned and since Kym knew she was going to have to rely on her a great deal for support, it was a small concession to do as she wished.

The move to Australia had worked well. Simon had been born there and Kym's mother had looked after the boy while Kym got a job. It might have gone on that way forever, she reflected now, as she opened the door of a steriliser to take out several instruments, if her mother had not suddenly begun to long to go back to England. The disease was catching, and eventually Kym had begun to yearn to be back in London. So, impulsively, they had returned, had settled into a small flat in West London, and Kym had started looking for a job once more.

One day in Oxford Street, coming out of Marks and Spencers, she had bumped into Gemma Page, a nurse who had worked on Wren with her all those years ago. Gemma had married, but was now divorced, and back at St Alphage's as a theatre sister. As always, the extrovert Gemma knew all the gossip.

They had lunch together, and Kym heard all about the new building, and the fortunes of various members of the staff she had known. Gemma urged her to go along and have a look at the new hospital.

'Call in and see Miss Cartwright,' she suggested. 'She'll be tickled pink to see you. You remember her? She was Sister on Wren—she's DNO now.'

Kym made a face. 'I was always getting on the wrong side of her.'

Gemma laughed. 'Who wasn't! She's mellowed quite a bit actually. Promotion improves some people.' It was her turn to pull a face. 'Not everyone, though. Remember Harley Garfield? Didn't you go around with him for a while?'

Kym nodded. She strove to keep her voice level. 'We went out together a few times.' She hoped Gemma had forgotten that silly dare the night of the Nurses' Ball.

It seemed she had, because she went on, 'Well, he's recently become a consultant physician, the youngest in hospital history, I believe. And arrogant with it, so some of the young doctors say. Jealousy, I expect. Our paths don't often cross, so I wouldn't know. But maybe the rapid rise in fortunes has gone to his head. I believe he also came into quite a considerable inheritance a year or so ago.' She laughed suddenly. 'The other doctors might resent him but there are still plenty of nurses willing to fall at his feet!'

'Is . . . isn't he married?' Kym had to ask the question.

Gemma shook her head. 'No. He's got the reputation of love them and leave them. Marriage isn't part of his master plan apparently.' She laughed again. 'You weren't in love with him yourself, were you?'

Kym flushed fleetingly, and denied it. 'No . . . of course not. Does he ever take a girl out for long enough for her to fall in love with him?' she queried with light sarcasm.

Gemma shrugged, and went on to talk about someone else.

It was at that meeting that the seed had been sown. Kym had kept turning over in her mind what Gemma had told her. Harley was doing well in his career, and apparently he now also had private means. He was still unmarried. Perhaps, she thought, for Simon's sake she ought to tell him about his son. He was quite obviously in a position to be able to do something for the boy when the need arose. Kym had already begun to worry about the future, Simon's education and career. She didn't want him to be deprived just because she was too proud to approach his father. She mulled over the notion for some time, alternately attracted to, and repulsed by it, until finally she decided that she would tell Harley he had a son. It should be easy enough to do now. Her own feelings were no longer involved.

So, before her resolve weakened, she had taken a taxi to St Alphage's Hospital, and marched up to the main entrance, intending to ask if she could either see him right away, or make an appointment.

Before she could do this, she had encountered Miss Cartwright, who happened to walk across the foyer as Kym entered. The Divisional Nursing Officer recognised Kym at once, and had shepherded her off to her office. Within half an hour she had persuaded Kym to return to nursing.

Kym explained to her that working in an office had paid better than nursing, and with a small son to support and unable to look to her mother for much financial help, nor wanting to, she had had to earn the best salary she could. Nurses' salaries were not as good as those in business, and besides, the hours were long and erratic, and she had wanted to spend as much time as possible with her baby.

Kym said doubtfully, 'I haven't nursed since I qualified.' She felt she would be totally inadequate after seven years away from her profession.

Miss Cartwright waved aside her doubts with firm reassurances. 'It doesn't matter. We'll give you a short refresher course and frankly, once you're on the wards again, it'll all come back. We won't expect too much of you at first, naturally. There'll be some new techniques for you to learn, I dare say, but I'm sure you'll pick things up quickly.' She had smiled confidently. 'You always did. You were an excellent nurse, Kym, and it's the profession's loss that you've stayed out of it for so long. But I sympathise with your reasons, of course. Any mother would have done the same.'

Kym, whose heart had always been in her first-chosen career, could not resist Miss Cartwright's persuasions, and besides, she saw at once that it might make the ordeal of approaching Harley easier. She would see him in the course of her work, and perhaps be able to judge the best moment to drop her bombshell.

Carrying the tray of instruments, Kym left the sterilisation room, not without a swift glance around her, with something like awe. It had never been like this in the old place, she thought, running her eyes over the sparkling autoclaves, and the dressings and instruments cupboards. It was all so light and bright, and cheerful. The old St Alphage's had been gloomy at the best of times.

In the corridor, she paused briefly to look out of a window. Wren ward was on the fourth floor and the corridor windows commanded a view across London that the narrow casements of the old hospital had never allowed. In one sweeping glance she could see Tower

Bridge, the dome of St Paul's in the distance beyond, and the Post Office Tower. There were other buildings, too, on the skyline, that had not been there when she went away. Nearer at hand pleasure steamers were chugging past, their wakes disturbing the glassy grey silk surface of the river Thames. Kym drew in a slow breath and let the feeling of deep pleasure that this scene engendered wash over her. She knew that she was, despite everything, happy to be back. Back in London, and back at St Alphage's.

She turned abruptly from the window, her thoughts sending her stomach into a nervous somersault once again, and at the same moment the double doors she had just come through were flung open. The edge of one clipped the tray she was carrying before she could step aside. She stumbled slightly, her foot slid from under her and she and the tray went down with a loud clatter. Above the noise she heard her own gasp of dismay, and hard on its heels a sharply muttered oath, followed by, 'For God's sake, Nurse, can't you look where you're going?'

The voice seemed to pinion her to the floor, unable to move, as she raised her eyes to his. Harley Garfield's deep-set blue-grey eyes regarded her with intense irritation, and he made no attempt to help her up. Kym sprawled helplessly at his feet, waiting tensely for the tirade of admonition that his face showed he was about to deliver to the clumsy newcomer on Wren ward. There was not a flicker of recognition in those steely eyes in that first moment.

But either something in her own expression jolted his memory, or it surfaced of its own accord. After an instant or two of staring at her blankly, he took a step towards her and said:

'Kym . . . ?' There was sheer disbelief in the question.

She nodded. 'Yes. H . . . hello, Harley.'

He held out his hand and she grasped it, scrambling to

her feet, smoothing down her uniform, and feeling a complete fool. This was not how she had envisaged their first encounter. She had imagined herself all poised and efficient, unflustered and calm, totally detached, and here she was thrown into total confusion, and stammering like a nervous first-year student.

'What are you doing here?' Harley asked incredulously. Kym had almost forgotten the deep rich tones of his voice, which now had the mellowness of maturity, and for a moment she could only let the words wash over her unanswered. He sounded accusing as he added, 'I heard you were in Australia.'

Kym was having difficulty finding her voice. It was a poor dried-up croak in the back of her throat, which any amount of hasty swallowing could not improve.

'I . . . we . . . came back,' she said at last, and went on in a rush. 'Mother was homesick . . . and I met Gemma Page in Oxford Street, and she told me about the new building, so I came down to have a look at it, and I bumped into Miss Cartwright . . . and she persuaded me to come back. Today's my first day,' she finished lamely.

His eyes had never left her face while she was speaking, and suddenly he seemed to realise that he still had hold of her hand, her left hand. She noticed his eyes resting for a moment on the ring on her third finger, but he said nothing. He let her hand go abruptly. Kym devoured his face with eager eyes. He had not changed much. There was evidence of maturity in his face as well as in his voice; a few fine lines radiated from his eyes and the creases at the corners of his mouth were deeper. He was as devastatingly handsome as he had always been, with his waving dark hair, swept back from a high forehead and curling slightly just above the collar of his white coat, and that shadowy, sensuous, slight cleft in his chin.

For an instant there seemed to be more than just recognition between them, a reaching out, a sharing remembered, and then it was gone. Kym knew it could only have been her imagination. His lips were as hard as his eyes. She remembered suddenly their softness, with a thrilling little shiver, and was instantly angry with herself for permitting the lapse.

'We're very short-staffed at the moment,' he said in an impersonal tone. 'You'll find yourself very busy.'

His manner was distant. Kym knew she ought to be glad. She wanted their new relationship to be as impersonal as possible. She could not go through with it otherwise. She had to forget that they had once been friends—and lovers. But suddenly she knew, with a heart-stopping spasm, that she was expecting too much of herself.

'I'd better see to this . . .' she faltered, glancing down at the floor, and feeling like a very green probationer under the scorch of his gaze.

'Yes, you'd better,' he agreed, and then to her surprise bent down, not to help retrieve any of the scattered instruments, but to pick up her cap which had flown off as she fell.

With a deliberate gesture, he set the scrap of blue-pleated linen jauntily on her dark curls. For a moment she held her breath as the light pressure of his fingers sent electric shocks spreading like wildfire under her skin. The memory of his touch long ago, of his fingers straying lightly down her cheek, encircling her neck, wandering through her hair, which had been longer before, made her tremble expectantly, but he took his hand away. Kym turned abruptly from him, kneeling swiftly to gather up the tray, not daring to look into those blue-grey eyes again. She heard his footsteps diminishing as he walked on down the corridor, and she knew with irrefutable certainty that she was not going to be able to tell him about Simon after all.

CHAPTER TWO

'I THOUGHT you must have got lost!' Sister Muir's jocular remark disguised the impatience Kym knew she must be feeling because of her long delay in returning with the tray of instruments. She must not try that patience too far, she thought, but she could not explain what had kept her.

'I'm sorry . . .' she said, inadequately. 'It took me longer than it should have.' She attempted a self-deprecating smile. 'I'm all thumbs . . . I . . . I dropped one or two things and had to sterilise them again.'

Sister Muir shrugged tolerantly. She hoped her leniency with the girl was not going to prove a mistake, and Wren ward find itself lumbered with a nurse who was inept and incapable of pulling her weight. Short staffing was a problem at the moment, it was true, but an inefficient nurse could cause more extra work for every-one else than no nurse at all.

She eyed Kym with some perplexity. Intuition told her that the DNO was right and Kym would prove her worth, but something was troubling the girl, and that could affect her work. It was probably something to do with her son, she decided. When the opportunity arose she must try to talk to her, get her to unwind a bit about her personal life. It might help all round.

Sister said, 'Well, never mind, but you'd better look sharp and set up the trolley. I'll double check it with you in a minute. Dr Garfield is always prompt and he's due here in a few minutes. I'd like you to come round with us this morning.' She glanced down the ward. 'You could start pulling the screens around beds two and eight. They're new admissions.'

Kym made a valiant effort to keep her mind exclusively on what she was doing. Nobody must guess that her edginess was due to the consultant physician who was about to do his rounds.

One of the other staff nurses came over to Kym, and said with a smile, 'Lucky you, going round with Dr G on your first day!' She rolled her eyes expressively.

'Lucky?' echoed Kym.

Nurse Susan Grant folded her arms across a shapely bosom.

'Everybody likes doing the rounds with Harley Garfield. If you don't do anything stupid like dropping spatulas and breaking thermometers when he's examining new patients, he'll probably favour you with one of his devastating smiles. He might even ask you for a date.' She looked Kym over with critical but kindly eyes. 'You're pretty and you've been married.'

Kym's eyebrows flew up. 'What's "married" got to do with it?' Her blood was racing warmly through her veins. She remembered how he had glanced at her hand, taking in the fact that she wore a ring, but not commenting on it.

Susan wrinkled her nose. 'He prefers married women, so they say! They're more experienced, and they're usually only out for a good time, not to trap him into matrimony! Of course, you're a widow and that's a bit different. He's probably wary of merry widows!'

Kym's cheeks began to burn, but Susan appeared not to notice, or to think anything of it if she did. She probably thought Kym was just easy to tease.

'Mind you,' she went on, 'He's aiming higher than mere staff nurses these days. He's been seen around quite a bit with the leggy, luscious, Lucinda Raymond, so the grapevine says. There's a bit of sour grapes about his getting a consultancy so soon. Most people think it was Lucinda's influence.'

Kym asked casually, 'Who's she?' and fought back the pang of jealousy that froze her blood momentarily.

Susan said, 'Of course you wouldn't know, would you, being new here. Lucinda is very classy. Daughter of the chairman of the hospital board.'

Kym had not yet told Susan that she had nursed at the old St Aphage's, so she did so now, adding, 'Actually I do remember Dr Raymond. He took a medical degree but never practised. He went into business instead. I don't remember his daughter though.'

'Raymond Pharmaceuticals expanded overnight into one of the biggest in Europe,' Susan told her. 'They've developed a couple of new broad-spectrum antibiotics recently. You might have heard about it. There's been some controversy about the side effects.'

'Yes, I believe I did read something about that,' Kym murmured absently. She was thinking that Harley was certainly moving up in the world if he was dating the chairman's daughter.

'Lucinda Raymond was married a year or so ago,' Susan continued, 'but it broke up almost immediately. Some wealthy American tycoon. It was all over the social pages—the wedding, and the divorce. I must say she's a stunner.' Susan was obviously more up-to-date on the details of Harley's life than Gemma had been.

Kym's smile was a trifle wry. 'Then I won't put too much store in a casual glance, devastating or not! He always was a flirt.' She regretted that last remark the moment it was said.

Susan looked momentarily surprised, then said, 'Of course, if you were here before, you must know him.' She added lightly, but with a shrewd glint in her eyes, 'Did he break your heart too?'

Kym was startled by the blunt question, and it took a moment to quell the rush of feeling that surged over her. 'No,' she answered firmly, taking a firm control of her emotions, 'I didn't know him all *that* well.' She forced herself to meet Susan's gaze unwaveringly, and hoped the girl believed her.

The last thing Kym wanted was gossip to go around that she had been thrown over by Dr Harley Garfield seven years ago, and was still smarting, especially as it wasn't true. Some astute person might just remember the Nurses' Ball when he had dared to enter the nurses' home and had spent the night in her room. She had had to put up with a fair bit of nodding and winking and teasing then, and she didn't want it to happen again. All at once she wished she had not been foolish enough to return to St Alphage's.

Susan glanced down the ward, and said in a low tone, 'Watch it, here he comes. Good luck!'

Their second encounter, to Kym's relief, was minus the drama of the first. He was accompanied by one of the registrars and both greeted her with a brisk, 'Good morning, Nurse!' Harley made no reference, even obliquely, to the incident in the corridor. He practically ignored her throughout their progress down the ward, dividing his attention between the patients, the registrar and Sister Muir. There hadn't been time for Sister to check the trolley and Kym waited apprehensively for Harley to find some fault, but to her relief he did not. Once she caught his eye but there was nothing in his expression to suggest that for him her return to St Alphage's held any significance, or that she had moved him to anything more than initial surprise.

She was just another woman in his life, as she had been before. The fact that he had been the most important man in hers, the only man with whom she had ever been so intimate, was something that would never occur to him, she felt sure, in a thousand years. There was no devastating smile for her when he took his leave. In fact he barely seemed to notice that she was still there.

Sister Muir said thoughtfully, after he'd gone, 'He's in a foul mood this morning. I've never known him so preoccupied. He's usually much breezier with the patients. I've known him to be quick-tempered when things aren't as efficient as he thinks they ought to be, but he isn't usually so brusque.'

'At least he didn't find fault with anything,' said Kym, thinking perhaps he'd had a row with Lucinda last night.

Sister Muir said, 'Thank goodness!' and added, glancing at her watch. 'You might as well go to lunch now, Nurse.'

Since she knew few people yet, Kym was pleased to see Gemma in the canteen. The breezy theatre nurse rushed over to her at the counter.

'Well . . . how'd it go?'

'All right,' Kym smiled hesitantly. 'It's all a bit strange . . . all the more so I think because I remember it being so different.'

Gemma grabbed her tray and dragged Kym over to a table. 'Did you see Harley this morning?' she asked with interest.

'Yes, I did,' Kym made an effort to sound uninterested.

Gemma was suppressing laughter. 'I remembered afterwards! It was you, wasn't it, who volunteered to smuggle him into the nurses' home that time. He spent the night in your room! We were all dying to know what happened, and you wouldn't tell . . .'

Kym's cheeks flamed. 'It was a silly prank . . . we were crazy. We nearly got caught, too.' She added quickly, 'I'd rather you didn't tell anyone about that, Gemma. It might—embarrass him.'

Gemma's expression feigned indignation. 'Of course I won't say anything!' Her laughter bubbled out. 'I can't help thinking about those days. We were a mad lot, weren't we?' She sighed reminiscently.

'I suppose we were,' Kym agreed soberly, wishing that they hadn't been.

Three other nurses joined them and the subject was dropped while Gemma enthusiastically introduced Kym. The conversation continued on current hospital topics until it was time for Kym to dash back to her ward.

The rest of the day flew past. Kym was rushed off her feet towards the end of her shift. They had had several new admissions that day and there was a minor crisis with an elderly patient who managed to dislodge his intravenous infusion. Kym had little time to think about Harley Garfield, which was just as well. It was not until she was going home on the underground that the pieces of her day began to fall into place, and she became more forcefully aware of what a ghastly mistake it had been to return to St Aphage's.

To make it worse, she had, in many respects, enjoyed her first day. Her return to nursing had not proved as difficult as she had feared. That was partly due to the refresher course she had attended, and the hurried studying she had forced herself to do, and partly that it was, as Miss Cartwright had predicted, merely a matter of getting back into her stride.

Almost immediately she had found herself doing certain routine tasks automatically, and, she realised with unexpected pleasure, really enjoying it. She had not been aware until now just how much she had missed the hustle and bustle of a busy ward, the dynamic atmosphere of a big hospital, and the feeling that what she was doing was truly worthwhile.

Temporarily her thoughts along those lines eclipsed thoughts of Harley Garfield, and it was not until she was travelling up the escalator at her station that the full impact of seeing him again really hit her. The feelings that she had so determinedly pushed aside all those years ago, that she had thought to be as non-existent now as her fictitious husband, had treacherously blossomed. Seeing him again had wrecked her resolve to tell Harley about his son, and had thrown her emotions into confusion, none of which was what she had expected or wanted.

Her mother regarded Kym anxiously when she arrived home. 'Was it all right?' she asked. A petite, pretty woman, despite her greying hair, Irene Andrews worried constantly about Kym, and made no secret of the fact that she would like to see her daughter marry and find happiness.

Kym kissed her. 'Of course it was!'

'Don't pretend to me,' said her mother, smiling with relief. 'You know perfectly well you were nervous. But you were glad to be back?'

Kym reflected briefly on her day. 'In many ways, yes. Although everything's changed. There are a few people I used to know still there, besides the DNO and Gemma. Not many though, at least so far as I've been able to discover.'

Simon ran into the room. 'Mummy . . .' He flung himself at her, and Kym hugged him, struck fleetingly by his likeness to Harley, something she had schooled herself to ignore ever since the day she had first held him in her arms and seen, with pain, the shock of dark hair and the grey-blue eyes that stayed that colour—the colour of his father's.

'I hope you've been a good boy today for Nan,' said Kym, smoothing the dark hair back, looking into the mischievous eyes. Even the young smiling mouth had a hint of Harley's about it, she thought suddenly, a suggestion of his independence and tough self-assurance, but with a belying softness, an underlying vulnerability.

'Of course I have,' the boy said. 'I was at school most of today anyway.'

'Did you learn a lot?'

'About animals mostly.' He looked up at her earnestly. 'I'm going to be an animal doctor.'

'You mean a veterinarian,' Kym pronounced the word slowly.

'That's right,' agreed Simon, 'a vertinarian!'

Kym and her mother laughed and Kym tousled the dark hair with affectionate fingers. It looked as though Simon might follow in his father's footsteps, even if at the moment it appeared to be only in the general direction.

That night, lying in bed staring into the darkness, Harley's dark head and searching gaze kept intruding, and wayward memories clouded Kym's thoughts. The long ago night in her room at the nurses' home was vividly to the forefront, every detail recalled. What a fool she had been not to realise that what had happened was what was bound to happen. But now, under the thin covering of the sheet her body trembled anew at the phantom touch of his hands and his warm vibrant flesh, as his body merged with hers, stirring her to heights of ecstasy she had never dreamed possible. But it was not just the physical contact she craved again. She had known the moment she had seen him again that she was still in love with Harley Garfield. That was why other men had seemed so unsatisfactory, and she had never felt even close to giving herself to anyone else. Harley had stolen her heart forever.

What distressed her now was that if she told Harley about Simon she might find herself having to see him often, and she was not sure she could bear that. It would be better if her secret remained a secret forever. She would have to leave St Alphage's and her first inclination was to run to Miss Cartwright the next day and tell her that coming back had been a mistake. She dreaded doing that. Miss Cartwright would think her silly and irresponsible and would expect her to at least give herself time to adjust. Since she could not explain her real reason for wanting to leave the day after she had returned, Kym had no alternative but to grin and bear it until she felt she could leave without letting anyone down, or looking a fool.

When she woke in the morning her pillow was still damp from the tears she had not been able to stem.

She went to work on leaden feet and with a heavy heart, knowing she would need all her strength not to let her feelings show, especially to Harley. She should have welcomed his indifference, she knew, but instead it hurt. It was easier to dislike him for his arrogance, which he displayed later that day.

Kym had answered the telephone and had taken a message confirming a 3.30 p.m. special appointment for Harley to examine a new patient. When he suddenly appeared in the ward unannounced, accompanied by a registrar, at two-thirty, she was taken by surprise. Unfortunately, his arrival coincided with Sister Muir's having gone along to the DNO's office to discuss some staffing matter. The first inkling Kym had of his arrival was to feel him breathing down her neck as she was taking some clean linen from the cupboard in order to make up one of the beds that had been vacated that day.

'Why isn't Mr Gregory prepared for examination?' a voice in her ear demanded, and Kym turned, startled, and so aghast she was momentarily lost for words. When she failed to answer, he went on in an autocratic tone, obviously irritated by her blank expression. 'Where is Sister?'

Kym coloured profusely because he had caught her off guard. 'Er . . . she's with the DNO,' she stammered, riveted by the steely grey-blue eyes that looked into her wavering blue ones with an expression of chill hostility. She wondered what she had done to deserve quite such a withering look.

'She is supposed to be here when I examine a new patient,' he said testily.

Kym was nettled by his arrogant manner. She glanced at her watch. 'I'm afraid you're an hour early,' she answered levelly.

He glowered at her for daring to contradict him, and glanced at his own watch. 'I said two-thirty, and it is twenty-five minutes to three.' The words were spoken in the tone of a man who never makes mistakes.

Kym insisted, 'Your secretary made the appointment

for *three*-thirty.' It was tantamount to arguing and a staff nurse did not argue with a consultant, even a comparatively recently elevated one.

'Who took the message?' he rapped out, unconvinced.

'I did!' replied Kym, on a defiant note.

Their eyes locked, his clearly showing irritation with what he evidently considered gross inefficiency, Kym's flashing with indignation. She was very annoyed, since she was certain he was the one in the wrong, but she sensed he would never admit it. He had certainly become a bit overbearing, she thought. It shouldn't take her long to get him out of her system if this was how he behaved.

'I'll phone through to the DNO's office for Sister, if you like,' Kym offered in cool tones, that she was afraid bordered on insolence. She couldn't help it. He had really riled her.

'Don't bother,' he said peremptorily, giving her another scorching look. 'I'll come back.'

Kym managed to maintain her calm although she was seething inside. Was this the father of her son? The man she imagined herself in love with? Obviously promotion had gone to his head.

When Sister Muir came back, she listened to Kym's account of what had happened and then shrugged. 'Well, as I didn't take the call . . .'

Kym felt badly about it. She was sure she had taken the message correctly, but there was no way of proving it. She felt that the incident made her look incompetent, and that Sister Muir was more likely to believe it was her error than the consultant's, or his secretary's. She simmered all afternoon, before, during and after his visit. He came back eventually, half an hour late, and Kym suspected that it was on purpose.

Although she tried to avoid him, Kym constantly found herself coming up against Dr Harley Garfield, and he made her so nervous she always seemed to do something silly to draw attention to herself which was the last thing she wanted.

Once, when she made a slip of the tongue in answering a question, and told him the drug dosage a colitis patient was having in grams instead of milligrams, he nearly hit the roof. He lectured her on the dangers of misreading instructions and confusing quantities, and ended by saying cuttingly, 'Anyone would think you hadn't qualified yet, Nurse! How long have you been nursing?'

Kay, smarting under the reprimand which she felt to be quite unjustified, replied in a wavering voice, 'I . . . I haven't nursed since I qualified. I've only recently come back to it.'

His eyes narrowed and there was an ironic twist to his mouth. 'Of course, I had forgotten. You were married— and you have a child . . .' She had not told him, so someone else must have.

He had never asked any personal questions, and he didn't now. He seemed to have no interest in what she had been doing since they had last met, and she said to herself, 'Why should he?'

One confrontation, however, disturbed her more than all the rest. It happened in the corridor one morning when she was late and hurrying along to her ward. Preoccupied, with her eyes on the floor, she didn't notice the two doctors standing talking in the middle of the corridor just ahead of her. One turned, and then paused to look back over his shoulder to say something to his colleague. He no more noticed Kym than she did him, and so they ran headlong into each other. It was Harley.

The collision knocked all the breath out of Kym. For one ghastly second she was caught hard against his chest, her chin bumping his breastbone. She lifted her face tremulously, expecting to see anger in the grey-blue eyes, but instead, to her horror, she saw an unmistakable kindling of desire.

It flamed there for a second, and then was gone, to be replaced by swift irritation.

'Don't you ever look where you're going, Nurse Rutherford?' he rapped out, pushing her away from him as though suddenly discovering she was infectious.

'I . . . I'm sorry,' she muttered. 'I was in a hurry . . .'

'Late?' The dark eyebrows lifted slightly, the tone was sarcastic.

She nodded sheepishly. Caught out again! He seemed to have a genius for it.

His head inclined slightly as he let his gaze rove over her from head to foot, and a humourless smile curved the full sensuous lips that she was trying to drag her eyes away from. 'Then I suggest you start out a little earlier in future. Or you'll be filling Casualty with your victims.' Cold, incisive as a finely-honed steel blade, his voice stabbed right into her heart, and his eyes showed no lingering of that earlier lapse.

That was the same day that Kym met Dr Joel Masters.

Gemma had persuaded her to go to a party that night. She hadn't wanted to but Gemma had insisted and bullied her into it.

'You must, Kym. It'll do you good. You've been out of circulation for too long. You look so morose all the time. It's bad for you. You can't mourn forever.'

Kym had protested, 'But I'm not . . . I mean . . .'

'No excuses,' said Gemma flatly. 'You are coming to this party if I have to drag you along by your hair!'

In spite of what she had said, Kym looked forward to the party and had even bought herself a new outfit for the occasion, a deep green silk crepe trouser suit that clung attractively to her shapely figure, and suited perfectly her creamy skin and glamorously upswept dark curls. With a little more eye make-up than usual and a faint touch of blusher on her cheekbones, she looked quite different to the girl in her trim but plain nurse's uniform. At the party she caused more than one pair of masculine eyes to turn, and one of these admirers approached her and Gemma.

'I don't think I've met your friend,' Dr Joel Masters said to Gemma, and smiled admiringly at Kym.

Gemma was delighted. She had been secretly hoping he would be attracted to Kym. She had paved the way tactfully by dropping a hint to him the day before. She had judged it would be better for him to make the first move rather than that she should insist on introducing Kym to him. Kym, she knew, was the kind of girl to resent matchmaking. However, seeing the wariness that flashed into Kym's eyes as she registered Joel's approval, Gemma crossed her fingers as she introduced them. After a few moments she drifted casually away.

Joel fetched Kym a drink and they chatted idly about St Alphage's and all that was new there since Kym had nursed in the old building. Joel had never seen it, having come to London only a year ago from the Midlands. When he offered to fetch her another drink and Kym handed him her empty glass, she saw his eyes alight briefly on the gold band on her wedding finger for the first time.

'You're married?' He said it in some surprise, for Gemma had told him nothing about Kym.

'I'm a widow,' Kym said, hating the lie, as lately she had come to hate it more and more. She added, a little defensively, 'And I have a five-year-old son.' Simon was six, but lately Kym had grown into the habit of telling people he was younger, so that no-one would start becoming too curious or start putting two and two together and connecting her departure from St A's with Simon. It was highly unlikely anyone would, while she hid behind the screen of being a widow, but Kym was very sensitive of the fact that there were still some people at St Alphage's who remembered her, and might recall her sudden departure.

There was no immediate flicker of dismay in Joel's

eyes as Kym had half expected there to be. She was
accustomed to that reaction from men. Instead he
looked her over slowly, then said with a smile, 'You
don't look old enough, or harassed enough to have a
five-year-old son.' He added gently, 'If I may say so you
are a very attractive young woman.'

'Thank you . . .' Kym felt slightly embarrassed, but
she liked this tall young doctor with the shock of reddish
brown hair and rather attractive hazel eyes. She spent
quite a lot of time talking to him during the evening,
either alone or in company with others, and he made her
feel at ease, something she had not often felt with a man
in recent years.

When he asked if he could drive her home, she
agreed. Gemma winked heavily at her as they were
leaving and whispered, 'I knew you two would get along
like a house on fire. Enjoy yourself!'

When he pulled up outside the house where Kym had
her flat, Joel turned to her and said hopefully, 'Do you
think your mother and son could spare you again soon?'

Kym hesitated. Part of her wanted desperately to go
out with Joel, to behave like a normal young woman,
instead of the recluse she had virtually become since
their return to England, but she was as wary of this
good-looking young doctor as she was of every man who
asked her out. She was tired of extricating herself from
unwanted embraces that threatened to go too far.

'I don't like leaving my mother to look after Simon too
often,' she said evasively.

'But surely, now and then . . .' he urged.

Kym did not know how to put him off without sounding stuffy or downright rude. 'Well, I suppose so . . .'
she said hesitantly.

'What about Friday next week?' He was quick to press
the advantage.

'Oh, I don't think so . . .'

'The week after?' he pursued with a smile.

Kym decided quite suddenly that she was probably being rather silly. Her mother was always urging her to go out more and enjoy herself. 'Well . . . perhaps I could make next Friday,' she said, and saw his face express genuine pleasure. It was very flattering.

'What about dinner and a show?' he asked, 'or perhaps a show first and a late supper might be nicer?'

'Whatever you like,' she said, 'thank you very much.'

'I'll call you,' he promised, and did no more than touch her hand briefly as he said, 'Goodnight, Kym. I had a very enjoyable evening—thanks to you.'

She could not reciprocate quite so wholeheartedly, even though he had been largely responsible for her own enjoyment, but she said lightly, 'Thank you for driving me home, Joel. I enjoyed the party too.'

Joel Masters telephoned her two days later and confirmed their date. He asked her what her preference was for shows on in the West End, and she said she hadn't seen any of them, so she would leave the choice to him.

When Friday arrived she almost wished she had not accepted Joel's invitation, already shrinking from even the slightest form of involvement with a man, long before any such possibility arose.

Her mother, of course, was delighted that she was at last embarking on some social life. It had worried her that since they had returned to England Kym seemed to have withdrawn further and further within herself. She had often noticed when Kym was unaware of her scrutiny, a growing unhappiness in the gentle blue eyes, and was disturbed by it because she did not know the reason.

'You ought to go out more,' she told Kym. 'You need some social life, and there's no need for you to worry about Simon. I don't mind looking after him. I have plenty of time to myself during the day now he's at school.'

Kym hugged her. 'You're marvellous, Mum. I shall never be able to repay you for all you've done.'

Irene's eyes clouded. 'You'll repay me everything the day you find some nice man and get married.' She added casually, obviously making an effort to conceal her intense interest, 'What's this Joel Masters like? A doctor, you said?'

'Yes. He's quite good-looking,' Kym answered with a laugh. 'A bit of a flirt perhaps. Not the sort of person I'm likely to get serious about.'

'Well, so long as you enjoy yourself, that's the main thing,' her mother said, not too disappointed by Kym's lack of enthusiasm. Anything could happen when they got to know each other better. She repeated, 'And don't worry about Simon. We'll find plenty to do to amuse ourselves any time you want to go out in the evening.'

On Friday Joel picked Kym up at home and announced with some satisfaction that he had got tickets for a show he felt sure she would enjoy.

'Something light and bright, and a bit of a brain-teaser,' he said. 'It's a comedy thriller.' His eyes ran lightly over her, and his smile was full of admiration. 'You look wonderful . . .'

Kym was pleased. Compliments didn't often come her way these days. She had felt very extravagant buying the blue dress she was wearing, since she had bought a new outfit only a short time before, but there was nothing in her meagre wardrobe that pleased her any more, and she did not want to wear the same dress for her date with Joel as she had worn to the party.

The blue dress had caught her eye because of its swirling pleated skirt and pin-tucked bodice. She had felt that the neckline was a little revealing, so she had pinned the edges together with a gold brooch to achieve a more demure effect. There was no point in inviting the very thing she did not want. The velvet jacket that went with the dress was in a darker but toning shade of blue. She had brushed her dark curls into a chic style and had taken a little longer over her make-up. It was not so much that she was out to impress Joel, as the fact that she had not been out on a date for quite a long while and the prospect was unexpectedly exciting.

She responded lightly, 'Thanks! You look better out of a white coat, too!'

They started off on the right foot, she mused later, mixing just the right note of levity, the right level of seriousness. The play helped. The plot was taut, it was brilliantly acted, and the audience alternated between laughter and being on the edge of their seats. Kym thoroughly enjoyed it and it certainly encouraged an easy-going atmosphere between them.

Afterwards they walked from the theatre to a restaurant near Leicester Square. The traffic, the lights, the hustle and bustle of West End nightlife all helped to make Kym feel exhilarated and her step was light. She was a little dismayed, however, when she saw that the restaurant Joel was taking her to was a rather select, expensive establishment. She glanced up at him warily.

He caught her arm and gave her a reassuring smile. 'I can only afford to come here because some friends of mine own it. We'll get VIP treatment and free champagne!'

Kym did not believe him at first, but she soon discovered that he was known to the head waiter, and the service at their table was certainly swift and unobtrusive. Champagne did indeed appear without their having asked for it. That Joel had been speaking the truth was finally confirmed when a glamorous woman came over to their table and lightly dropped a kiss on his forehead.

'Joel, darling,' she said in warm husky tones. 'We haven't seen you for ages. Where have you been? Charles said only yesterday that we must give you a tinkle.'

Joel said, 'Marion . . . I'd like you to meet a friend of mine, Kym Rutherford. She's a nurse at St Alphage's.'

To Kym he said, 'Marion and Charles Forbes are very good friends of mine.'

Marion smiled at Kym. 'The most ravishing yet, Joel,' she said, lightly teasing. 'Your taste is improving!' Speaking to Kym, she advised, 'Don't take him too seriously. Joel Masters is a heartbreaker.'

'Don't pay any heed to her,' said Joel, twinkling. 'She's just jealous!'

There was more light banter, then Marion Forbes drifted away on a waft of expensive perfume. Across the room she stopped to speak to a tall, distinguished man in a dinner suit. 'That's Charles,' Joel whispered. 'I expect he'll come over for a chat shortly.' He added a trifle ruefully, 'He's a friend of my father's and ever since I came to London, they've sort of taken me under their wing. They feel duty bound to approve of my girl-friends—or disapprove!'

Kym said teasingly, 'Do you bring all your girlfriends here?'

He laughed. 'Only the ones I know they'll approve of! Marion's a dear and Charles has been very good to me. I guess I wouldn't get married without their approval.' He gave a low chuckle. 'But I've no plans to get married yet awhile.'

Kym had been wondering how long it would take him to make that point. Well, that's telling me, she thought wryly. Joel sounded just like Harley Garfield.

'What do you plan to do?' she asked with interest.

'Surgery,' he confided. 'It's hit me recently that that's what I really want to specialise in.'

They talked of medicine and hospitals for a while and Joel was keen to hear of developments in Australia. Kym, however, was only able to tell him what she knew secondhand from reading medical journals, since she had not actually worked in hospitals in Australia.

Although she was engrossed in their conversation, Kym found her attention drawn all at once towards a couple who had just come into the restaurant and were being shown to a table on the other side of the room. She caught her breath as she recognised Harley Garfield. With him was a tall, languid blonde. Lucinda Raymond, she presumed.

Joel noticed them too. 'Hello . . .' he said softly. 'Our ambitious young consultant and his latest conquest.'

Kym could not stem the colour that swept into her face, nor could she help saying, 'I've heard that some of the young doctors are jealous of his rapid progress.'

Joel looked a little quizzical at her defensive tone. He said, 'He is the youngest consultant St A's has had, and dating the chairman of the Board's daughter to boot isn't bad sort of homework. His career won't stumble over any obstacles you can be sure. I guess we all wish we had his magic touch.'

'They make a handsome couple,' Kym remarked, not realising how drily.

Joel gave her another swift, and curious look. 'Don't you like him either?'

Kym avoided the trap. 'I don't know him very well,' she evaded, 'and I try to be impartial about superiors if I can.'

'Very wise,' Joel approved. 'Too many personal likes and dislikes get in the way of hospital efficiency, but it's human nature, I suppose. Personality clashes are inevitable.'

Kym sensed a more personal grudge than just envy. 'You and Dr Garfield don't hit it off?' she suggested.

'There was an incident,' he admitted, 'nothing to get steamed up about, I suppose, but I resented his arrogant attitude.' He grinned. 'However, like you, I try to remain strictly impartial!'

For the remainder of their meal, Kym found her eyes straying across the room, unwillingly but involuntarily. Harley and his companion were more in her line of vision than Joel's. She could not help but be aware of the girl he was with, or observing that she was beautiful, sophisticated and clearly very taken up with Harley. Her long, fluttering eyelashes were visible even from a distance, and Kym did not doubt that the eyes behind them were adoring.

Having started their supper ahead of the other pair, Joel and Kym were ready to leave before them, and had to pass their table on their way out. Out of politeness they paused to say hello.

Harley glanced at Kym and then at Joel, but his face registered no particular surprise or interest.

'Good evening, Kym,' he said. 'Joel . . .' He turned his head. 'I don't think you know Lucinda . . . Lucinda Raymond.' He introduced Kym as 'a former St Alphage's nurse who has recently returned after several years in Australia'.

It was a brief, courteous exchange, introductions really being superfluous, Kym thought, since she and Joel were not joining the other couple, and it was unlikely that either of them would meet Lucinda again. When they were outside, after a prolonged farewell with Marion and Charles, who made Joel promise to come back soon 'with your lovely companion', Joel said:

'I suppose Harley Garfield thinks he can afford someone like Lucinda Raymond now.'

'Are you envious?' Kym inquired lightly.

He slipped his arm around her waist. 'No. He'll pay for what he gets, you can bet on it. She's got eyes like blue diamonds, cold and hard, and underneath I'll wager there's a very calculating heart.'

'I've got blue eyes,' rejoined Kym accusingly, with a teasing smile.

He looked down into them, rather disconcertingly. 'But not a calculating heart,' he said.

Joel drove her home and to her relief expected no more than a kiss. He asked her if she would go out with him again, and Kym said yes she would like to.

CHAPTER THREE

THE DAY after her date with Joel Masters, Kym met Harley in the lift. She was just going on duty, and had not yet changed from her outdoor clothes to uniform. He had evidently just arrived, as she had. He caught the lift doors just as they were closing, and held them open.

Their eyes met. Kym felt herself crumbling tremulously inside at the sight of him. She wished he could have arrived a few seconds later and so allowed her to miss him.

'Good morning.' He favoured her with a faint smile, then went on in a rather formal tone, 'Did you enjoy yourself last night?'

Kym was surprised at the inquiry, and also the noticeable softening of his manner. 'Yes, I did, thank you. Did you?' The doors had already slid across, enclosing them in an enforced intimacy that made Kym feel uncomfortable.

'It's a very good restaurant,' he answered, his eyes continuing to hold hers, in a speculative way.

The lift stopped at her floor and the doors opened. Harley held them apart with one hand and lightly detained Kym with the other. She glanced up at him questioningly, and then received the shock of her life.

'Would you be free this evening?' he asked. 'For dinner.'

Kym's mouth fell open. The leap from indifference to this was sudden to say the least. 'Th . . . this evening,' she echoed. 'Oh, I don't think I could . . .'

'Tomorrow then?' he persisted. As though feeling his invitation needed an explanation, he added, 'It's a long time since you went away. A lot of water has flowed under the bridge.' His eyes drifted briefly to the gold band on her left hand, and Kym supposed it was only natural that he should be curious about her. It was just that he had shown no interest so far, and it was a shock to find his attitude changed.

There were many things she wanted to ask him too, but just the thought of going out to dinner with him, alone, set her emotions in such a turmoil she knew she must not do it. She refused as politely as possible. 'I'm sorry . . . I have another engagement.'

'The day after?' His steely blue-grey gaze searched her face. He knew she was making excuses.

Kym gritted her teeth. She had no intention of dating Dr Garfield. It was bad enough having to see him in the course of her work. She was in a situation she should never have allowed herself to get into, but she had to put up with it for a little while longer, before she could extricate herself on some plausible pretext. Even then she was going to feel a heel, and she dreaded what Miss Cartwright would say. Sister Muir too. They would think her very unreliable.

'I'm sorry,' she said again, very firmly this time. 'I really haven't an evening to spare.'

His eyebrows quirked. 'Perhaps you should consult your diary,' he suggested. 'I can book ahead.'

His look shredded her heart and she could hardly bear it. Now he was flirting openly with her, as he had before, but this time she wasn't going to be taken in. If only he didn't send her emotions into such a turmoil every time she set eyes on him.

'I'm sorry,' she repeated. If only he knew what an effort it was for her to say no! 'I am rather busy, and I don't like to leave my mother alone too often.'

He was not used to being rebuffed so bluntly, and his displeasure showed clearly in his face. He answered coolly, 'As you wish,' and let go of the doors. They closed on him, and Kym broke into a run, hurrying along to the nurses' room, biting back tears of anger, frustration and love that threatened to spoil her composure.

She slipped hastily out of her ordinary clothes, noticing that she was a few minutes late, and flung on her crisp blue uniform with its dark blue cuffs and belt. As she adjusted the cap on her curls with a quick, impatient gesture, she fleetingly recalled the feel of Harley's fingers on her hair that first morning when she had dropped the instrument tray and he had picked up her cap and adjusted it for her.

'I must stop this foolishness,' she told herself severely as she sped along the corridor to Wren ward. 'It's ridiculous! I should never have come back. I must have been crazy!' She tried to tell herself, as she had done many times already, that she had done it only for Simon, but she knew very well that wanting to see Harley again had played a big part in her decision to return to St Alphage's to nurse.

Sister Fremlin was on duty this morning, and she was not as friendly and understanding as Sister Muir. She glowered at Kym over her horn-rimmed spectacles and, hands on her solid hips, frowned disapprovingly.

'Nurse Rutherford, do you always have to charge about as though you were dashing for a train? I like my nurses to be brisk and efficient, not laggards, but I do wish you'd give yourself a little more time . . '

Kym cringed before her. 'It's the first time I've been late this week,' she ventured, feeling she did not entirely deserve the rebuke.

Sister Fremlin pursed her lips. She preferred nurses not to defend themselves. 'And the last, I trust,' she retorted frostily. She added, 'The DNO will be bringing some visitors around this morning, so I want you to make sure everything is shipshape. Some of the bedside tables are very untidy. And you'd better see if anyone wants anything and attend to them right away. We don't want anyone ringing for a bedpan when there are visitors on the ward.'

Kym felt like saying, why not, since this was a hospital after all, and patients couldn't be expected to organise their bodily functions just to suit visitors, but she knew it would never do, so she said meekly, 'Yes, Sister,' and went obediently to do as she had been told.

Sue, balancing a bedpan like a waitress with a drinks tray, paused to have a word with Kym. 'The old dragon's on the warpath this morning,' she hissed in Kym's ear. 'Very important visitors apparently. Not quite Royalty, but almost.' She laughed. 'You should have been here when the place was officially opened and the Queen was coming. It was a riot. I thought they were even going to whitewash the patients at one stage! And rumour had it that the Gremlin had a new uniform specially made at Hartnells!'

Kym laughed. It was inevitable that Sister Fremlin should be nicknamed the Gremlin, and the notion of her going for fittings for a new uniform to one of the royal dressmakers, was picturesque to say the least. Some of her tenseness disappeared. Susan's good humour always helped to cheer the day.

There was a certain amount of expectancy in the ward as the patients learned of the visit later in the morning. Most of them welcomed the minor diversion, and some hoped they would be chosen for a passing word or two, but a few were always resentful of being put on show, and Kym had quite an argument with Mr Rushton who declared it was an imposition, an infringement of a person's rights, and that sick people ought not to be paraded like a circus, and that he was going to get up and go into the day room.

He was suffering from a chronic respiratory condition and was not well enough to get up. He was liable to need oxygen at any time, and Kym explained that it was not convenient to move the oxygen apparatus into the day room. He argued with her for some minutes, growing more and more petulant while she tidied his bed and bedside table.

'As if it isn't enough for a sick person to put up with, you nurses coming round shoving thermometers in our mouths, needles in our arms . . .' he grumbled.

'Now, Mr Rushton,' soothed Kym, plumping up his pillows and rearranging them in the position most comfortable for him, 'you'd complain all the more if we didn't look after you. The visitors will only be here for a few minutes.'

'Too long,' he complained, and closed his eyes, setting his mouth in a stubborn line. 'They needn't stop and talk to me,' he muttered rebelliously.

Kym looked down at the cantankerous old man with pursed lips and gave a small sigh. Then she smiled. She quite liked Mr Rushton, really. He wasn't always cranky and not as much trouble to nurse as he sometimes seemed. He liked to chat to someone about the old days, and usually it was her because she didn't mind stopping to listen to him. Sister Fremlin had remarked once or twice that she shouldn't let the patients engage her in conversation so much, but Kym ignored that advice. If anyone wanted to talk, and she had time, she felt it was an important part of her duty to listen.

By the time the visitors arrived, the ward was as neat as a new pin, with every bedside table ship-shape, flowers refreshed, and counterpanes smoothed down just so. Miss Cartwright accompanied the small group of visiting overseas health officers, and also in the party was Harley. Kym could not help thinking, as she watched the group pause to be greeted by Sister Fremlin, how distinguished he looked. Her heart beat quickened, and her cheeks began to feel uncomfortably warm when Harley caught her eye. There was an odd expression in his eyes that she could not fathom. All she knew was that she was possessed of an almost irresistible desire to rush into his arms. What a sensation that would cause, she thought!

She was as glad in the end as Mr Rushton when the party had passed down the ward and, after stopping to speak to one or two patients, disappeared through the double glass doors at the other end. Seeing Harley was becoming a more and more unnerving experience. There must be some way, she anguished, to make it not matter.

Since he had already been that day, Kym was not expecting another visit from Dr Garfield, but he appeared unexpectedly in the ward that afternoon. Sister Fremlin was taking her coffee break in the canteen for once, and as she happened to be near the door when he entered, Kym was the nurse who greeted him.

'Good afternoon, Dr Garfield,' she said, not quite meeting his eyes, and struggling to quieten the fluttering of her heart.

He acknowledged with a cursory nod. 'I just popped along to check on your peptic ulcer case. Mr Poynter isn't it?'

'Yes . . . that's right.'

'His wife telephoned me. Evidently she is not happy with the way he is being cared for.' Kym was forced to look at him. She knew he could not fail to see the outrage in her face.

'And what exactly is she complaining about?' she asked in a brittle tone.

A quiver of a smile moved his lips before he said, 'Nothing specific. Just that he isn't getting well quite as rapidly as she expected. I tried to explain that his condition may not improve rapidly, but that he is receiving the very best nursing care. Nevertheless, I had to promise to come down myself and check on the patient.'

Slightly mollified, Kym said, 'I think Mr Poynter might be asleep at the moment. Would you like to look at his notes?'

'Yes, I would, thank you,' Harley said, moving down the ward. When Kym lingered, intending to get the case notes out of the file for him, he turned his head. 'Come with me. I might want you to answer a few questions.'

Kym followed him reluctantly. He was much pleasanter to her now than he had been at first, but he still disturbed her dreadfully and she wished he would go away, leave St A's and put her out of her misery. Being near him was worse every time it happened. She could not help noticing the smiles that greeted him as he walked along the row of beds, saying a word here, a word there. The patients all adored him and even old Mr Rushton greeted him in a friendly way, despite the fact that it was to complain about the 'invasion this morning, dashed nerve, you know we're powerless to object'. As they passed his bed, Harley turned to exchange an amused glance with Kym and the instant of shared understanding inexplicably warmed her. His manner towards her had certainly changed dramatically and she wondered why.

At Mr Poynter's bed they paused. The patient was not asleep as Kym had thought he might be, and he too greeted Dr Garfield warmly. Harley's questions were casual but precise. He was obviously being careful not to alarm the man by his special visit and it was doubtful whether Mr Poynter did in fact realise it was a special visit. Harley glanced at the chart Kym handed him, but made no examination of the patient other than taking his pulse and asking a few casual questions.

'Getting enough to eat are you?' he asked, smiling. 'Not bored with your diet?'

'Nothing wrong with the food here,' declared Mr Poynter, and with his hand half over his mouth, said confidentially, 'To tell you the truth, doctor, it's a damned sight better than I get at home, but don't breathe a word to my wife, will you?'

'Certainly not!' said Harley, and exchanged another

swift understanding look with Kym. 'Quite satisfied with the service are you?'

The elderly man grinned. 'Best holiday I've had in years.' He looked a bit anxious. 'I'm not well enough to go home yet, am I?'

'No, not yet,' agreed Harley. 'I'm afraid it's quite a slow process. Peptic ulcers are no joke, but you're coming along nicely and there's nothing to worry about. With a bit of luck you won't need to have an operation.'

'Mollie worries,' said Mr Poynter gravely. 'She thinks I should have been up and out of here by now, or having an operation. I told her, but . . .' he sighed. 'She always did think I was swinging the lead if there was anything wrong with me.'

As they were walking back up the ward, Harley said, 'He's happy anyway. A not uncommon situation. She wants him home because she's missing him, although she doesn't want to admit it. People miss each other sometimes, even when they don't get on all that well.'

'She can't be much of a cook,' remarked Kym, 'if he prefers hospital food to home cooking.'

There was sudden laughter in his eyes, as he accused, 'You are not knocking hospital food, Nurse, I hope!'

'Well, a peptic ulcer diet is scarcely gourmet,' she replied, suddenly feeling a little bit more at ease with him.

'I suspect Mollie's cooking aggravated his ulcers,' said Harley, as they paused at the office door. 'Too much fish and chips and suet pudding!'

Kym laughed. 'Do you still want to see his notes? It won't take a minute to fetch them out of the file.'

He shook his head. 'I don't think that will be necessary.' He did not go but stood there looking at her until she began to feel uncomfortable again. At last he said, 'No cancellations?'

Kym was puzzled. 'Cancellations?'

His lips formed a faintly ironic smile. 'In your diary.'

The surprise attack caught her off-guard and she flushed in sudden confusion. But she retained enough presence of mind to say quite firmly, 'No.'

He shrugged. 'You needn't bother to tell Sister I barged in unannounced. You know what a fuss she'll make over implied criticism.'

He turned and left Kym staring after him, a constriction in her throat that almost hurt.

'I wish we'd stayed in Australia,' she murmured fiercely to herself, as she thumped one fist into her other palm. 'Oh, I wish we'd never come back . . . and I wish I'd never been stupid enough to come back here . . .'

It had been all right in Australia, she thought, as she answered a patient's call for more lemon barley water. There, she had been able to put it all out of her mind—almost. She had come to terms with the situation, at any rate. But coming back had been a mistake, and coming back to St A's had been an even bigger one. Harley Garfield was on her mind day and night now, and it didn't help to see his features in miniature every time she went home and Simon flung himself enthusiastically into her arms. Despite his maturity, Harley still retained traces of the madcap boyishness she had once found so endearing, and under the devil-may-care personality he flaunted in his private life, and the brisk efficiency he maintained in his professional life, a certain vulnerability lurked. Simon was going to be like him, she thought regretfully.

Perhaps she should have said she would go out with him, she thought several times. Perhaps that would have been the way to erase him from her system once and for all. But she was afraid to face the danger that it would not be the solution, but would only make matters worse. And she had no intention of becoming Harley Garfield's temporary lover. She was not foolish enough to hope that she could make it permanent if she told him about Simon. She was determined not to fall into that trap. It was better not to have anything to do with him personally. She must just be patient. As soon as she decently could, she would disappear from St Alphage's and start again somewhere else. She had done it before, she could do it again.

Meanwhile she continued to go out with Joel Masters and occasionally with other men if they asked her. There were always parties on the go, and although she was not a great lover of parties, she found they gave her social contact without involvement. Harley was never at any of the parties she went to, and he never asked her out again.

Kym enjoyed Joel's company in particular. He was very undemanding, and had put their relationship on a purely temporary non-involved footing right from the start. She didn't blame him for that. Men were always wary of a girl with a child. Naturally they thought she was looking for someone to support them. She and Joel went sometimes to the same parties, and they also formed a fairly regular habit of meeting one or two evenings a week in a small riverside pub that had loads of atmosphere, good food, and the kind of music they both liked. It was casual and fun, and sometimes others from St Alphage's would be there too. Joel always drove her home.

In case one or the other was held up and unable to make contact beforehand at the hospital, their arrangement was to wait half an hour for each other. It was more often than not Joel who was held up, having been called to deal with some emergency, but Kym did not mind that. Being a doctor or a nurse one had to put up with quite a lot of inconvenience and frustration from time to time.

One evening when it appeared that Joel was not coming, Kym was just thinking that she would go when she had finished her drink, since there was no-one else there she knew, and she had waited three quarters of an hour, when to her surprise, because she had never seen him at the Ship and Gun before, a familiar figure entered the lounge bar. It was Harley Garfield. He saw her at once and strode straight over to the corner where she was sitting.

'All alone?' he seemed surprised and there was a slightly mocking edge to his tone. He glanced around the bar, perhaps expecting to see her escort there somewhere.

'I was just going,' she said, half rising. 'I was supposed to be meeting a friend but he hasn't turned up.'

His eyebrows rose slightly. 'Poor show!'

'Oh, it often happens,' she said lightly, 'when you date a doctor.'

The grey-blue eyes narrowed. 'Masters I suppose,' he said, and there was clear dislike in the mention of Joel's name.

Kym squared her shoulders. 'As a matter of fact, yes. He must have been delayed.' She started to edge out from behind the table, but Harley leaned across and pushed her back into her seat. Caught off balance she slumped back onto the bench with an annoyed gasp. 'Oh!'

He said, 'You might as well finish your drink.'

'It's a bit flat and warm,' she said, starting to get up again.

'Then I'll buy you a fresh one,' he offered.

'No . . .' she began to protest, irritated by his autocratic manner.

He fixed her with an accusing gaze. 'I haven't got the pox,' he said in a harsh tone. 'And you can scarcely be in a hurry if you were planning to spend the evening with Dr Masters.' His expression changed suddenly and he treated her to what Sue on Wren ward called his devastating smile.

Kym felt her heart turn over, and bit her lip. She slumped back in the seat again, letting him win.

'Is that cider?' he asked calmly.

'Yes . . . but this will do,' she said, thoroughly flustered now.

'On your own admission it's flat and warm,' he reminded her. 'I'll get you a fresh one. Sweet or dry?'

'The . . . er . . . dry one, thank you,' she said, unable to make her words come out smoothly.

Kym watched helplessly as he went over to the bar and ordered the drinks. Her stomach was churning, partly with nerves and partly with a strange kind of joy. Wanting to be with him, not wanting to be within miles of him, was a conflict she knew she would never resolve.

He strolled back, looking darker and more saturnine in the dim light than in the bright white light of the wards. The shadows accentuated the lines in his face and the cleft in his chin, and intensified the strong uncompromising line of his jaw. He placed the glasses on the table, then sat opposite her. She kept her legs tucked away under the seat to avoid even accidentally touching his under the table.

'Well . . .' he said, raising his pint of beer, 'here we are . . . cheers!'

'Cheers . . .' Her voice sounded cracked to her own ears, betraying her inner turmoil, but he gave no sign of noticing anything odd about her manner. She rushed on, 'I haven't seen you in here before.'

'No. It was done up a couple of years ago, but it hasn't been one of my haunts. Somebody mentioned it to me the other day so I thought I'd drop in and see what it was like.' His eyes strayed to her left hand and the gold band on her third finger. He was evidently very curious about her marriage because he asked straight away, 'How long have you been a widow?'

'Several years.' She looked down into her drink lest he should suspect the lie.

'But you're getting over it now?'

Kym resented the inquest. She looked up sharply. 'As well as one ever gets over losing someone.' That wasn't a lie. She had lost him, hadn't she, as finally as if he had died?

'You have a young son, I believe.'

So he had been picking up bits about her on the grapevine. 'Yes. His name's Simon.' As she told him, there was that odd twinge of guilt she had felt before, that Harley had a right to know . . .

'It must be difficult, bringing up a child alone,' Harley said, revealing an underlying sympathy beneath the inquisitive tone.

'It has its problems,' admitted Kym, 'but thousands of single parents manage it.' She added loyally, 'My mother has been a great support to me.'

'I never met your mother,' he said reflectively, with what sounded almost like disappointment.

Kym found her eyes suddenly locked with his as she said, 'No—we weren't that friendly, were we?'

He gave a short private laugh, and his eyes burned into hers. 'No, I suppose we weren't.'

There was a charged silence. Kym sipped her drink and tried not to think about that night seven years ago. She wondered if he was thinking of it too. If so, it would only be as one night amongst many. There had no doubt been many more like it, before, and since, with other girls. There had been nothing special about it for him to engrave it on his memory as it had been engraved on hers.

He spoke suddenly. 'What made you go to Australia? It was quite a sudden decision, wasn't it?'

Kym did not want to talk about it, not to him of all people, but there seemed no alternative short of getting up and leaving, which he had already twice prevented her from doing. 'Not all that sudden,' she said, 'we have relatives out there and we had been thinking about it for quite a while. After my father died my mother was very restless and I thought a change of scene would do her good.'

'And you . . .'

'Oh, I was always keen to travel. You knew that,' she said blithely.

'Did you like Australia?'

'Very much.'

She wished he would not regard her so intently. It was like an inquisition.

'You met your husband out there?'

'Yes.'

'He was killed in a car accident.'

So he had found out that much about her. But why did she have the feeling he didn't believe it? 'Yes.' Tears came unbidden into her eyes, but not for the reason he naturally thought.

'I'm sorry . . .' He reached across and touched her hand briefly, making her tremble inside, and her eyes brim even more. 'It was thoughtless of me to probe. I'm sorry, Kym.'

Relieved that at least he had misinterpreted her emotion, she wiped her eyes, annoyed with herself for so weakly showing her feelings. 'I don't talk about it if I can help it,' she said. That at least was true.

'Then we won't.' His hand reached out again, this time to close over hers which was fiddling with the unused ashtray. He squeezed her fingers gently, and apologetically. 'You're even prettier than I remember, Kym.' He laughed reminiscently. 'You were always so bright and bouncy, so full of energy and life, and anxious for everyone to be happy. Attentive was a word I heard used about you once in connection with your work. Of course, you've matured . . . and experience has moulded you, but there's still a trace of the old Kym left!'

'You flatter me!' she remarked drily, trying to withdraw her hand, but he seemed not to notice. Any minute now, she thought, he's going to remind me of that night, the silly escapade, and we're going to laugh self-consciously about it, and I'm going to break up inside all over again . . .

But he did not mention it. He glanced at his watch. 'Seeing your date has stood you up, you might as well let me buy you some dinner. This is a dreary place to renew our acquaintanceship.'

'No, really, I'd rather not . . .' Kym said, resisting with some difficulty.

The darkening eyes narrowed again. 'You say no so often that I might be tempted to believe you really mean yes,' he said. 'I can't believe you dislike me so much you can't bear to have dinner with me.'

Kym said wearily, 'Do you always get your own way?'

His fingers slid between hers, gripping tightly, and he smiled a little too devastatingly for her composure. 'In my position, I need to be a bit autocratic.' There was a glimmer of mischief in his eyes. 'And I find that women usually like domineering males!' He stood up, pulling her to her feet as he did so. 'Come on, I don't know about you, but I'm starving. I didn't have time for lunch today.'

Kym gave in. He was too strong willed for her, and she wanted so much to spin out this time with him. 'All right,' she whispered. She only hoped she wouldn't regret it.

CHAPTER FOUR

HARLEY took Kym to a small Italian restaurant on the fringe of Soho, downstairs into a dimly lit interior where the tables were tucked into secluded cubicles, and there were red-checked tablecloths, candles spilling wax over their wine bottle holders, straw-covered chianti bottles on the walls in clusters, and posters of Roman ruins. The waiters were swarthy Latins and their flashing dark eyes admired Kym openly. It was an intimate, romantic sort of place, Kym immediately wondered if Harley ever brought Lucinda here. Somehow she thought not. It would not be quite her style.

A man was playing an accordion in a far corner, but the music was subdued and did not intrude on their conversation, which Kym endeavoured to keep to 'shop'. She did, however, dare to ask Harley a little about himself, since he had inquired into her personal life.

'What have you been doing these past few years?' she asked, after they had started their meal. 'Besides rising to be one of the youngest consultants St Alphage's has ever had.'

He scoffed modestly. 'They were hard up for someone, that's all! All the best doctors have emigrated!' He laughed, then added offhandedly, 'I studied a fair bit, and I did a two-year stint in the States. I learnt a lot about modern medicine, and didn't care for some of it. I can see the day when patients become mere digits on a computer programme if we aren't careful. We'll have to fight to keep humanity in the hospitals.'

'You're not in favour of computerised medicine, then?' she suggested.

'Don't get me wrong! There are things a computer can do that boggle the mind, and their capacity for time-saving often means life-saving, but I don't believe in dehumanising medicine.'

'Robot nurses,' said Kym, with a teasing smile, 'might be rather less fun!'

He grinned. 'We've already got a few! I've heard it said the Gremlin has stainless steel hips and a plaster of Paris bosom!'

'Unkind!'

'But not you, Kym . . .' There was a look in his eyes that she had seen before, and it scared her, although it was only to be expected, she supposed. He had desired her once, so was it strange he should desire her again? She had been a fool to come with him, she realised, but there was plenty of time to avoid an awkward situation. She would make sure he didn't drive her home. It seemed strange thinking thus about a man who was the father of her son, and she could not help the wayward thought: 'He could have been my husband.'

Presently a dark-haired girl wearing a frilly blouse and colourful gathered skirt stopped by their table. She was carrying a basket of red carnations, and she asked Harley if he would like one for his companion. He glanced at Kym who shook her head, but he took no notice.

'Thank you,' he said, taking the flower and paying the girl. She flashed him a smile that was openly flirtatious, and strolled to the next table. Harley handed the flower to Kym, who felt embarrassed. This was not the kind of date where a man bought a flower for a girl.

'You shouldn't have . . .' she said, seeing no alternative but to accept the flower gracefully.

Harley just smiled, rather enigmatically and lifted the bottle of wine out of the ice bucket to refill her glass. Kym hastily placed her hand over the rim.

'No . . . I've had enough, thank you. It was very nice. You finish it.'

Watching him raise his glass to his lips, she was suddenly tempted to ask the question that she most wanted answered. 'I'm surprised you're not married, Harley.'

'Are you?' The blue-grey eyes were shadowy in the candlelight, and seemed to taunt her a little.

'Well, not really, I suppose,' she conceded. 'You always said you were more interested in a career than marriage, that you didn't want to be tied down. But people change sometimes. Now you've achieved most of the things you set out to do . . .'

'You think I ought to be dreaming of slippers by the fireside and the patter of tiny feet?'

'Are you?'

He took time to answer. 'Perhaps, if the right woman came along . . .'

'You have an ideal woman?' Kym asked, a trifle shortly.

He smiled a slow teasing smile. 'Oh, yes, she's cute, blonde, buxom, willing . . .'

Kym cut in crossly. 'Be serious.'

He let his eyes rove lazily over her, still half teasingly. 'I met her once and didn't realise it until it was too late.' The teasing faded from his eyes and was replaced by a shadow of regret. Kym suddenly felt sorry for him.

'And she married someone else?' Kym hazarded.

'Yes . . . as a matter of fact she did.'

'Maybe you'll meet someone else one day.'

'I hope so,' he said, then, shifting his chair, 'I think it's about time I took you home. It's getting rather late and I know you start early.'

Kym said, 'It's my day off tomorrow,' then wished she hadn't as it looked as though she wanted to prolong the evening. Outside on the pavement she quickly corrected that impression. 'It was a lovely meal, Harley, and I enjoyed talking to you very much, but there's no need for you to see me home. The tube station's just across the road and I can be home in no time.'

He grasped her arm. 'I have never allowed a young lady I have taken out for the evening to go home alone,' he declared. 'I would feel utterly responsible even if you only tripped and laddered your tights!'

'Don't be silly, Harley,' Kym protested, wrenching away from him. 'I'll be perfectly all right.'

'I am still taking you home,' he rejoined, regaining his hold of her, and putting authority into his tone. 'Do your other escorts allow you to travel home alone on the underground?'

'Well . . . no, not usually.'

'Don't quibble. Of course they don't. Now, let's not stand here arguing. The car isn't far away.'

In desperation Kym again wrested her arm away from him, saying, hotly, 'Don't be such a bully! You're not at St A's now! I am going home by tube and that's that!'

What happened next was something Kym never clearly remembered in detail. She started across the street, practically running in her anxiety, dodging recklessly between taxis and other cars, only to find her hand suddenly caught by Harley just as they reached the opposite pavement. At the same moment a young couple bounded off the kerb, forcing them apart again. Kym could afterwards only remember flashing coloured lights and a loud explosive sound in her ears.

The next thing she knew Harley was standing over her and she was lying on an unfamiliar couch in an unfamiliar room. Her first thought was relief that she wasn't in hospital. Trying to sit up, she asked anxiously, 'What happened?'

'You walked into a lamp post!'

Kym felt her forehead and found a cool compress on it. Her head felt wuzzy so she sank back on the pillow that had been supporting it.

Harley said, 'You dodged to one side as we were crossing the road, to avoid bumping into a couple of young idiots, and you ran straight into a lamp post. You knocked yourself out cold.'

Kym let her gaze drift muzzily around the large high-ceilinged room with its ornate cornices. She could see red velvet drapes drawn across some of the windows, the glow of lovingly polished antique furniture, the glimmer of reflections in silver and brass.

'Where am I?' she whispered, although she had a pretty shrewd idea.

'I'm afraid I had no idea where you lived,' said Harley, 'so the easiest thing to do was to bring you home with me. I wasn't sure how seriously you'd hurt yourself.'

Kym sat up and the room swam alarmingly. She subsided. 'My mother will be worried,' she said weakly.

He sat down beside her, taking her hand in his. 'No she won't. I'm afraid I took the liberty of looking inside your handbag for your address and telephone number. I telephoned her a while ago and told her what had happened. She's quite happy for you to stay the night here.'

'Stay the night here! I can't do that!' exclaimed Kym.

'You might as well. There's no point in disturbing your mother again at two in the morning, which it now is. If you feel up to moving, though, you might find it more comfortable to sleep in the guest room. Do you think you can stand?'

Kym's head was clearing. 'Harley, this is ridiculous,' she protested. 'I can't stay here.'

'I see no reason why not,' he said, and placed his arm under her shoulders to help her up. 'All right? Feeling dizzy?'

'A bit . . . no, it isn't so bad now,' she admitted.

'Good. I don't think you've done any real damage. Just a very mild concussion. You'll be as right as rain in the morning. You might have a bit of a shiner though.'

He touched the edge of her left eye tenderly and she winced. There was a painful spot right on the bone. 'Hmmm . . .'

He was getting his own way again, she thought resentfully, as he walked her across the room. And the ironic part was that if she hadn't objected to his driving her home, she wouldn't be here—which was infinitely worse. Near the door she stumbled and he tightened his hold then, in a sudden unexpected movement swept her up into his arms, saying, 'I think this will be easier.'

He carried her bodily up the stairs to the guest room, where the bed was already turned down. There was a frilly nightgown lying across the pillow. For some reason she recoiled from it.

'My sister's,' he said blithely. 'Half her clothes are here while she's away in Saudi Arabia. She's a doctor too, you know.'

Kym didn't know. She didn't know very much about this man at all, she thought, except that he was her son's father. A sudden overwhelming desire to tell him came over her and she almost succumbed to it, and might have done if he hadn't said briskly, 'I'll fetch you a warm milk drink. Undress and get into bed while I'm gone. The bathroom's over there.' He pointed to a door on the other side of the room.

It was crazy, she thought, bizarre even, to be donning his sister's nightie (was it hers, or was he just saying that? Maybe it belonged to Lucinda or some other girl who stayed regularly) and slipping between the sheets in a bed in his house.

He was back within a few minutes with a tray and a glass of warm milk and a couple of pills. 'Doctor's orders!' he said with a smile, and waited while she swallowed the pills and drank the milk.

'You'll be fine in the morning,' he promised. Deliberately he bent over her, shifting some strands of her hair on the pillow and looking into her face. 'You know, of all the girls I've known, you're the one I've most remembered.'

She turned her head away. She did not want to hear such things. They were meaningless and false and with one object in mind. Like seven years ago when during the night he had murmured 'I love you' but hadn't really meant it. His lips now burned her cheek and his fingers pulled her face around so that she had to look at him.

'Kym . . .' his voice was husky. 'Surely you remember too . . .'

'No!' The protest was never uttered because his lips were on hers, seeking, probing, exciting her first with their softness, then stirring her more deeply with their hard urgency, and even her anger at his flagrant taking advantage of her weakened state was dissipated by the waves of pleasure his touch was generating.

At last he lifted his mouth from hers, but slowly and reluctantly. 'As sweet as ever,' he murmured, and his long fingers stroked her cheek, straying lightly over the soft sensitive skin below her ear.

'Harley . . .'

'Shhh,' he said softly. 'You need to sleep. Goodnight . . . or rather, good morning!'

He switched out the light and Kym knew nothing more until she woke to find the sunlight streaming in through the window. For a moment she thought she was at home, until turning she saw the strange clock on the bedside table, and panicked. It was nine o'clock. She sat bolt upright and looked around the room. Swiftly it all came back, and with it horror at the situation she had landed herself in.

She flung back the lilac sheet and swung her legs to the floor, pausing as a momentary dizziness assailed her. She stood up tentatively and walked across the deep pile lilac carpet on rather wobbly legs to the dressing table.

'Oh . . . no!' she gasped, looking in the mirror. Her left eye was black, blue and yellow all round, and there was a small graze just above her eyebrow. She touched her face gingerly. It was sore but not painful and fortunately her head did not ache.

She walked to the window on slightly steadier legs and looked out. She was on the second floor of an elegant house overlooking a leafy square with iron railings around it. Pigeons were waddling along the footpath, and there was a blackbird scolding some unseen opposition from the railings. A woman was leisurely walking a slow overweight dachshund. Kym turned back into the room wondering what to do. There was a négligé on the chair so she put it on and went to the door.

As she opened it, she saw Harley coming up the stairs, bearing a tray. He was wearing a black and gold striped silk dressing gown, and his hair was tousled and slightly damp. He must have only recently got up and showered since he was obviously not wearing pyjamas, Kym noticed. Her gaze rested briefly on the lightly haired expanse of his chest that the open neck of the dressing gown revealed. He stopped and smiled at her, and for a moment they both stood immobile, each taking the other in. Harley seemed rather bemused, Kym felt embarrassed.

'Oh, good, you're up. I was just bringing you some breakfast . . .' He glanced down at the tray. 'Do you like orange juice, cereal, toast and coffee? I can rustle up something cooked if you like.'

'No . . . please, that's marvellous . . .' Kym said, and stepped forward to take the tray from him. It was a bit like a play, she suddenly thought, when the actors have forgotten their lines and the prompt has gone home, and they have to make it up as they go along.

'I had no idea it was so late,' she said, 'I overslept . . . I must phone . . .'

'Not to worry,' he said cheerfully. 'It's your day off, remember? And I've phoned your mother again to say you're all right, and will be home later.'

Kym had forgotten it was her day off. She heaved a sigh of relief. At least she wouldn't be in trouble at St Alphage's. And Harley had taken care of her mother. He was very thoughtful, she had to say that for him.

'You think of everything,' she said, weakly, reaching out for the tray.

He said, 'Since you're up, and feeling okay, why don't you come down and have breakfast with me?'

She was very conscious of the fact that she was still in her night attire, that the négligé was flimsy, and that he appeared to be wearing only his dressing gown, but as he had already started back down the stairs, she really had no option but to comply.

She followed him down the deep red-carpeted staircase, admiring the collection of original water-colours on the wall. There was a general air of affluence about the house with its antique furniture, original paintings and deep pile carpets. She could not resist remarking on it.

'This is a beautiful house,' she ventured as they entered the morning room which had french windows opening onto a sunny patio where a Siamese cat was sprawled lazily washing himself on a cane lounge.

Harley said, 'It was my grandmother's. I am very fortunate to have inherited it. She had exceedingly good taste as well as the means to indulge it.' He glanced around. 'It isn't all to my liking, but I haven't had time yet to make my mark on it.'

'I think it's just beautiful,' sighed Kym with undisguised admiration. 'I wouldn't touch a thing if it were mine!'

He laughed. 'I doubt that. Every woman likes to impress her own personality on a house. You'd make a few changes, I'm sure.'

Kym wished she had not made her remark. It now seemed presumptuous and she was afraid he might have taken it the wrong way. She walked through the open windows and bent to stroke the cat, who looked up at her

with inscrutable blue eyes and seemed about to withdraw from her touch, but changed its mind and nuzzled
her fingers with its nose and chin, then rolled over onto
its back, inviting her to tickle its tummy.

Harley appeared behind her. 'You're a hit! Kai
doesn't often let a stranger do that. Come and have your
breakfast. The coffee will be cold.'

Kym followed him back inside the house. 'You have a
beautiful garden, too,' she remarked, moving towards
the table where Harley had placed her tray. Opposite
was another tray, presumably his breakfast.

He caught her shoulders to detain her, and turned her
to face him. She shivered at his touch, self-consciously
aware that she was clad only in a nightdress and an
almost transparent négligé

'Let me look at your eye.' His sensitive physician's
fingers tilted her chin and touched her eye and the slight
swelling around it. His face was close to hers and she
could feel her heart thundering wildly despite her effort
to remain calm.

'Hmmm . . . quite colourful, but not serious,' he
pronounced. Then, looking at her seriously, 'How's the
head?'

'Fine, I don't feel any dizziness now.'

'Headache?'

'No.'

'Good. If you get the slightest suggestion of a
headache, in the next few days, promise you'll see me at
once?'

Kym promised. His hands dropped to her shoulders
and stayed there for a moment or two. His mouth curved
in a slightly bemused smile, and he shook his head and
heaved a sigh. Then he let her go, saying, 'As I said, the
coffee will be getting cold.'

Kym sat down. 'I'm sorry you've been so put out,
Harley,' she apologised hesitantly. 'It was very kind of
you . . .'

'Think nothing of it,' he rejoined dismissively.

Kym had just noticed the creamy white rosebud that lay on her tray. She glanced up as he smiled, saying, 'You lost your carnation last night, so I picked you a rose instead.'

'Thank you . . .' She wished he had not done that. It was a romantic gesture and there could be no romance for her and Harley. She had made up her mind about that. And yet, she could not help being foolishly touched.

'I'm sure I must be holding you up,' she said, pouring coffee, and trying to be matter-of-fact.

His smile was electric and made her heart turn over. 'Not at all. It happens to be my day off too today.'

Kym only half believed him. 'I expect you had something planned,' she said, feeling guilty.

'As a matter of fact I hadn't. I was just going to have a nice lazy day pottering in the garden.' He glanced at his watch. 'Come on, eat up, and then I'll take you home in case your mother starts to think I've abducted you.'

Kym finished her breakfast and offered to wash the dishes, feeling she ought to do something to repay him.

He brushed her offer aside. 'No need. My housekeeper will be here shortly. Mrs White will take care of it.'

'Oh.' Kym felt she had made a blunder not realising he was bound to have domestic help.

'I'm very lucky having Mrs White,' Harley said. 'She lives about five minutes away, and she comes in daily. She keeps the house like a new pin and cooks me delicious surprises which she leaves with simple instructions for simple-minded bachelors to follow.' He laughed. 'She's almost as good as a wife.'

'Won't she be curious about the two trays?' Kym asked.

Harley's features crinkled into amusement, and he arched one eyebrow mockingly. 'I shouldn't think so.'

Kym flinched. He was telling her she wasn't the only one to have had breakfast with him. An image of Lucinda Raymond flashed across her mind. No doubt she had breakfasted here too.

'Do you really have a sister?' she asked pointedly.

His laughter rippled around the room. 'You are suspicious! Yes, I do. Her name's Marianne, and she really is a doctor. Usually she lives in a flat in London but she gave it up when she went to Saudi Arabia and burdened me with all her belongings. She stays here, naturally, when she comes home.'

Kym felt rather small. She had not meant to show her lack of trust so openly, or to let him see that she had only half believed the clothes she was wearing belonged to his sister. To make it worse he was laughing at her because of it.

She got up from the table and insisted that at least she could take the trays back to the kitchen. Harley allowed her to do that much.

'Now I'd better get dressed,' she said on her return, anxious to escape as soon as possible from his disturbing presence.

She took a quick shower in the lilac-tiled recess in the en suite bathroom, and dried herself on the fluffy lilac towel laid out for her use. Then she quickly dressed, hesitated for a moment over what to do about the rumpled bed, then gave a shrug and left it unmade. Doubtless that would be what she was expected to do. She cast a lingering look around the room before she left it. It was so tastefully decorated and furnished, she felt quite envious.

Harley was reading the paper on the patio when she appeared, the cat curled up in his lap. He was wearing casual grey slacks now and a wine coloured shirt under a navy blazer. His hair was brushed back smoothly, and in profile he looked very handsome and distinguished. He looked up and grinned at Kym.

'You're not going to be able to get St A's to believe how you got that shiner, you know!'

Kym pulled a face. 'I know! Don't rub it in. I'll be teased unmercifully, I suppose.'

'Especially if they know you were with me.'

'I won't mention that,' Kym assured him quickly, sensing that her reassurance was what he was hinting at.

His eyes held hers briefly. 'That's entirely up to you.' He folded his newspaper and tucked it under a cushion. The cat shifted on his lap as he moved, stood up and arched its back, stretching luxuriously.

'Come along, Kai, down you get,' Harley said, running his fingers down the cat's back and along its waving tail. 'Time for pond therapy!'

'What on earth's pond therapy?' asked Kym, amused.

'Siamese cats are very highly strung,' explained Harley, deadpan, 'so Kai spends a couple of hours a day watching the goldfish in the garden pond. A friend of mine who's a psychiatrist suggested it. It prevents nervous twitches.'

'Doesn't he catch the goldfish?' asked Kym.

'Never. He's too lazy, you see, and besides the water is just out of reach because we have neighbouring fisher-cats who are more adept than he is.'

'I would have thought it would frustrate him rather than relax him,' said Kym, matching his mock serious tone.

Harley shook his head. 'No. Kai just likes to watch them swimming around, while he daydreams. Off you go, Kai.'

The cat took a long speculative look at Kym and then obediently strolled off down the garden, waving his tail, presumably towards the pond. Kym laughed loudly. 'For heaven's sake!'

Harley joined in her laughter. 'You don't believe me, do you?'

'You're crazy,' she said, 'you always were a bit mad.'

She stopped, her gaze held fast by his. For a moment there had been a normality between them that came from having known each other before. And yet nothing was the slightest bit normal any more.

Harley touched her arm, 'Ready?'

'Yes . . .' She hesitated. 'Look, Harley, I can manage to get home without bothering you.'

'Stop being so infuriatingly independent,' he said with a trace of irritation. 'If you hadn't been so argumentative last night you probably wouldn't have bashed your head.'

Kym had to agree with that. So she meekly acquiesced to his driving her home. As she sank once more into the luxurious upholstery of his sleek grey Volvo, she allowed the thought to cross her mind yet again—what a pity Harley was a confirmed bachelor. What a pity he hadn't fallen in love . . .

In less than half an hour Harley was drawing up outside the house where Kym had her flat. As she turned to thank him for everything once again, out of the corner of her eye she spotted two figures coming along the street.

'Oh, no!' she breathed silently.

It was her mother and Simon, and they were the last people she wanted Harley to meet. She must get rid of him before they came up to the car.

Hurriedly she opened the car door. 'Well, thanks very much for everything,' she said briskly. 'I mustn't keep you any longer.'

But she was not quick enough. Before she could slam the door, Simon, who had spotted her and broken into a run, was dashing along the pavement calling, 'Mummy!'

Harley was saying, 'I'd like to meet your mother and your little boy, Kym,' and he was getting out of the car, too.

CHAPTER FIVE

As Simon flung himself into Kym's arms, Harley came round the car towards them.

'Gosh, Mummy, what a terrific eye!' exclaimed Simon, more in admiration than sympathy.

'Darling . . . are you all right?' Irene Andrews came up to her daughter, her face creased with anxiety. 'I've been so worried about you.' She smiled warmly at Harley. 'You're Dr Garfield? I must thank you very much for taking care of Kym.'

'It was a pleasure,' he said gallantly, adding, with hand extended, 'How do you do, Mrs Andrews.'

Kym watched his devastating smile's effect on her mother, with wry amusement. Harley certainly possessed an effortless charm; but she could not help a feeling of uneasiness. Surely her mother would notice the resemblance between Harley and Simon. Kym knew she must have mentioned Harley's name when she was going out with him all those years ago, but of course she had had other boyfriends and it was possible it would not mean anything to her mother. She certainly showed no sign of remembering at the moment.

Kym glanced at Harley. She was not really afraid that he would see his own features reflected in the boy who was looking up at him with frank interest. People seldom recognised a likeness to themselves in another person, and especially in a child. And as Harley had no reason to suspect that Simon was other than the child of Kym's marriage to an Australian, the thought would never cross his mind.

Harley said cheerfully, shaking Simon's hand, 'So

you're Simon. I've heard quite a bit about you. You're going to be a vet, is that right?'

Simon looked pleased. 'Yes, I am.' Then he turned shy suddenly and scuttled behind Kym, who said, 'We really mustn't delay you any longer, Harley. You've been terribly kind . . .'

'Perhaps Dr Garfield would like a cup of coffee,' put in her mother hospitably. Kym could have kicked her for saying that.

She nevertheless expected that Harley would refuse, but he surprised her again by graciously accepting the invitation. There was nothing Kym could do but endure it. It was painful in the extreme sitting there in her own sparsely furnished living room, with Harley sprawled at one end of the couch pretending, or so she felt, deep interest in Simon's drawings of horses and cows and other animals. The boy had got over his bout of shyness and, under gentle coaxing from Harley, had opened up, as easily captivated by Harley's charm as her mother. He was even calling him Uncle Harley!

'You have quite a way with children, Dr Garfield,' Irene said as she brought in the coffee and chocolate cake. 'I suppose you have a family of your own?'

He said a trifle wistfully. 'No. I'm afraid I seem to be a perennial bachelor.' He insisted, 'Please call me Harley.'

'Oh, what a shame,' said Irene sympathetically, while Kym privately mused that Harley did not need or appreciate sympathy on that score. Irene went on, 'You'd make such a good father, I'm sure. Still, perhaps one of these days you'll settle down.' She shot a swift look at Kym, which Kym fervently hoped Harley did not notice. Matchmaking mothers, she thought grimly, even when you're as fond of one of them as I am, can be dreadfully embarrassing.

'Harley isn't the marrying kind,' Kym said, and was

aware of the faint note of bitterness in her voice, which she hoped he was not.

Simon interrupted at that point, but he did not improve the situation at all. 'Uncle Harley,' he said, 'are you coming to the zoo with us?'

Harley glanced at Kym. 'Zoo?'

Kym had quite forgotten. 'Oh dear,' she said, 'I'm afraid it slipped my mind. I promised to take him to the zoo today. He's been asking ever since we got back from Australia.'

Irene put in anxiously, 'Do you think you ought to, Kym, dear? It might be wiser to spend the rest of the day quietly resting. What do you think, Dr . . . Harley?'

Simon set up a wail of disappointment as he realised that the promised treat was not going to eventuate. 'But you promised!' he cried.

'Now, Simon,' rebuked Irene. 'There's no need to make such a fuss. Mummy isn't feeling very well, and the zoo will keep until another day.'

'I was looking forward to it,' grumbled Simon pouting.

Kym gave him a hug. 'So was I, pet, but you wouldn't like everyone staring at us because of my eye, would you?'

Harley said, 'I think Mummy should rest today, Simon. She had a nasty bump on her head and her eye is probably rather painful.'

Simon reached up and touched the bruise very gently. 'Is it sore?'

'Only a bit now.'

He heaved a sigh. 'Oh, all right.' Then, 'Can we go next weekend?'

'Yes, darling, of course,' Kym promised.

Simon looked at Harley expectantly. 'Will you be coming too, Uncle Harley?'

There was a flicker of surprise in Harley's eyes, since he obviously had not expected to be invited.

Kym said hastily, rather embarrassed, 'Uncle Harley is a very busy man, Simon. He hasn't got time to . . .'

Harley cut her short. 'If I'm invited, I'd love to come. It's years since I went to the zoo and I believe it's changed a lot.' His eyes met Kym's with a glint of something she could not quite make out, but it made her feel uneasy. The last thing she wanted was to spend the day with Simon and Harley, like a family group. 'Well, Kym, am I invited along?' he persisted.

Kym did not know how to get out of it. She realised that she would have to agree now, and perhaps think of some excuse later. 'Yes . . . yes, of course if you'd like to,' she said, but without a great deal of enthusiasm. He might, of course, cry off himself, later, when he realised she did not want him along.

Although pressed by Irene, he refused to stay for lunch, and for this Kym was grateful. When he had gone Irene was all smiles and enthusiasm. 'What a thoroughly nice man!' she exclaimed. 'But I thought you were seeing Joel last night. You haven't finished with him, have you?'

'No, Mum, and don't start jumping to conclusions, please, where Harley is concerned.' She explained what had happened briefly, finishing, 'He did what he thought was for the best, that's all. He was just being kind.'

Irene eyed her daughter suspiciously. 'I don't know. He seemed very keen to go to the zoo with you and Simon next week.'

'That, I am sure, was impetuous, and he will regret it and cry off during the week,' said Kym, thoroughly convinced herself that it would be so. 'He's got better things to do than to trail around the zoo with one of his nurses and her kid.'

'He seems fond of children,' persisted her mother.

'He was probably flattered by Simon's attentions,' suggested Kym. 'But whatever the reason, I assure you there's nothing to get excited about. I know you, darling, you see every man who takes me out as a potential husband. You'd like nothing better than to marry me off, but, let's face it, most men don't want a woman who already has a child, and especially when they find out the truth about me. And I wouldn't marry anyone without telling the truth. Besides, I don't want to get married.'

'You're still deeply in love with Simon's father, aren't you?' observed Irene quietly.

Colour flooded into Kym's cheeks. She was terrified her mother would guess the truth, so she said quickly, 'Can't we change the subject, Mum?'

Irene patted her arm. 'Yes . . . I'm sorry, love, I shouldn't harp, but . . . well, Simon needs a father now more than he ever did.' She looked at Kym appealingly.

'I can't help it,' Kym replied, too sharply. 'Plenty of people do without and they don't all become maladjusted or delinquent. I'm doing the best I can for him. If you think I'm not . . .' Tears were starting in her eyes and she could not go on.

Irene slipped a comforting arm around her shoulders. 'Kym, I'm sorry, so sorry . . . I shouldn't have said that. I didn't mean it as a criticism. Of course you're doing your best for Simon, and I'm proud of the way you've handled things.' She paused. 'It's just that lately, well, I wonder sometimes if we did the right thing coming back to England. You've been a bit edgy and not your usual bright self. I admit I've been wondering if you didn't come back solely to please me, and you'd really be happier out there.'

Kym hugged her. 'Mum, don't be silly. I wanted to come back too and I'm happy to be back. Truly I am. But it hasn't been easy going back to nursing. I'm not sure I should have after all those years away.'

'But you love it . . .'

'Yes, but it's hard to adjust and I've still got a lot to learn, to catch up on.' She was only telling half truths, but she dared not let her mother suspect that her edginess was to do with Harley Garfield.

'Well, darling,' said Irene practically, 'if it's too arduous for you, why don't you go back to office work again?'

'I might just do that,' Kym said. 'We could do with the extra money. But I can't leave St Alphage's just yet. I've got to give them a fair go. We're terribly short of nurses at the moment.'

Irene sighed. 'You must do what you feel is best, love I always felt your heart was in nursing, and I wasn't suggesting you went back to an office job because we can't manage. We do manage quite well really.'

Kym wanted to end the discussion. There were too many painful associations flitting through her mind. 'I think I'd better go and lie down for a while,' she said. 'My head's a bit wuzzy again. Don't worry about any lunch for me. I'll have a snack later.'

As Kym anticipated, there were a few teasing remarks in the ward about her black eye, and laughing disbelief at her story of running into a lamp post. She did not mention that she had been with Harley Garfield at the time. She guessed he would prefer her not to.

When she saw Joel briefly later in the day, he was full of concern and apologies. 'It was all my fault,' he groaned. 'If the car hadn't broken down . . .'

'Well, it'll teach me to look where I'm going,' Kym said ruefully.

He squeezed her hand. 'You shouldn't be allowed out on your own!'

Kym suffered no after effects from her bump, and the swelling subsided quite quickly, the bruise taking a little longer to disperse. In the days following the incident she saw Harley only when he came through the ward on his regular round, or if there was a particular reason for him to come at another time, such as the admission of a new patient needing prompt examination.

The first time he glanced at her eye and said quietly, 'No ill effects?'

'None.'

'That's good.' He went on his way, saying nothing about the arrangement to go to the zoo that coming weekend. It was possible, Kym thought, he had quite forgotten it. She resolved not to mention it herself.

But on Friday she was called to the phone during the morning and to her surprise she heard his warm vibrant tones flowing into her ear.

'Kym? Harley here . . .'

'Oh, yes, hello.' He must have just remembered, she thought, and was about to make his excuses.

'About Saturday.'

Kym said quickly, 'It's quite all right, Harley. I understand if you can't make it.'

'Now wait a minute,' he said, 'that wasn't what I was going to say. I'll pick you up at ten. Unless that's too early?'

Kym felt her heart lift, then plummet. Why was she letting him do this to her? 'All right, ten will be fine,' she agreed.

'See you then.' The receiver was replaced and she was left with only the echo of his voice in her head as she slowly replaced her end. She had made a mistake in not putting him off herself. She shrugged resignedly. This would be the one and only time, she vowed.

Kym tried to persuade her mother to come with them, but Irene would not be talked into it.

'No dear, I'm afraid I might be developing a cold, so I'll take it easy today. Anyway, you young things don't want a slow old body like me trailing along.'

'Mum, you know we'd love to have you,' Kym protested. 'I'm sure Harley will say you've got to come.'

'He can say what he likes,' her mother declared firmly,

'but I am staying home today! I don't want to get the 'flu. As a doctor and a nurse you should both agree with me.'

Kym was not sure whether her mother's excuse was genuine, or simply that she was anxious for them to go out alone. She did not press her any further, but she could not help feeling that having her mother along would have made things easier. Being together with Harley and his son was bound to be a disturbing experience.

At precisely ten o'clock she heard, with a slightly quaking heart, the hooting of the Volvo's horn. Simon was jumping up and down with excitement, and Kym suspected that it was because, for once, he was going to enjoy adult male company. Her mother was right, of course. A boy needed a father, especially when he started growing up. The terrible irony was that Simon and his father were about to spend the day together, unbeknown to anyone but Kym. The secret weighed heavily on her. What if she blurted out the truth? Kym shuddered. She must not. It could only cause more distress in the long run. It was better that Harley never knew. And yet deep down there stirred a faint niggling guilt—that he had a right to know.

The outing was a great success—at least Simon declared it was the best day he'd ever had and Harley tactfully agreed with him. Kym's feelings were rather more ambivalent, but she had to admit that there were moments when she had enjoyed herself despite the crazy circumstances. She had laughed a lot with them, and occasionally caught herself forgetting that it was a bizarre situation, and half believing they were just like any of the other family groups strolling around looking at the elephants, the monkeys, and all the other zoo attractions.

Harley had brought a camera, and Simon was thrilled to be allowed to take pictures of some of the animals.

'You shouldn't let him waste the film,' said Kym.

Harley squashed her protest. 'I want to finish the film up. It's got some shots on it I want to get developed quickly, so he's not wasting it.' He called to Simon. 'Hey, what about taking one of us?'

'No . . .' Kym objected, but Harley's arm was around her shoulders and he was bidding her smile.

'Now I'll take one of you and your mother,' said Harley obligingly.

There was only one exposure left after that, and Simon insisted on asking a passer-by to take one of all three of them. Kym felt embarrassed, and all churned up inside. Harley seemed not in the least put out because it made them look like a family group. He promised to give Simon the prints the very next time he saw him.

Simon was exhausted by the time they went home, and he fell asleep on the back seat of the car.

As they drew up outside the flat, Kym said, 'You've treated us to a splendid day, Harley. Simon had a wonderful time.'

'And you?' he queried quietly, staying the hand she had reached out to wake her son.

'Of course . . . I enjoyed it too,' she said, rather stiffly.

'Then you'll round it off by having dinner with me?'

She had to summon all her willpower to reply firmly, 'No . . . really I mustn't. You've done too much already.'

His gaze was piercing, seeking the truth. 'You have another engagement?'

'No . . .'

'Then why the hesitation?' he demanded.

Kym lowered her eyes. 'Harley . . . I . . . I don't want to get involved,' she stated bluntly.

His hand rested lightly on hers and two fingers drummed restlessly on the back of her hand. 'Who said anything about involvement? I'm not the marrying kind, remember?'

Kym blushed. 'I . . . I wasn't thinking of marriage. I just meant, well, let's face it, Harley, you do have a reputation, and frankly I don't want to end up just another one of your women.'

He sat back, stung by her words if his expression was anything to go by. 'You're wrong, Kym. I'm not half the man the gossips make me out to be! Oh, sure, I like female company. I am a man after all, and I'm not pretending I've been celibate or anything crazy like that. In fact I admit I would like nothing better than to whisk you off to bed right now, you're so very desirable, but I hope there's a little more to me than that. I enjoy your company. You're serious, and you're fun. You've got a mind where most girls have got fairyfloss, and it stimulates me.' He paused, eyeing her narrowly. 'That long speech means that if you'll have dinner with me, I'll promise not to try and seduce you!'

Kym had to laugh. He knew how to wheedle and no mistake. 'All right, you win,' she said. 'I have a feeling you always get your own way, don't you?' She added seriously, 'But a promise is a promise.'

'Cross my heart! Now, let me help you to shift this sleepyhead.'

'Do I need to change?' Kym asked, wondering where he intended taking her.

He looked her over. 'No. I know a little place in the country where jeans and sweaters are perfectly acceptable. We'll drive straight out there.'

'Well, we both need a wash and brush up,' said Kym. 'You can do it here if you like.'

'Great. It'll save time if I don't have to go home first myself.'

Simon stirred and grumbled because they were home already. He was a little put out when he discovered that he was to have tea alone with his grandmother because his mother and Harley were going out again, but Harley mollified him by promising to take them to Madame

Tussauds and the Planetarium the following week.

'I shouldn't let you,' Kym said later, as they were driving out of London.

'What?'

'Play uncles.'

Harley shrugged. 'Why not? He's a nice kid. I like him. We had fun, didn't we?'

Maybe you like him because he's yours, Kym wanted to blurt out there and then, but she stopped herself. Where would a confession leave her? Already she was storing up hurt for herself by allowing Harley into her life even to this degree. No more dates after this one, she vowed. Simon must not grow accustomed to him, and neither must she. She knew she could not bear having him around as a part-time father.

Over dinner Harley suddenly asked, 'You go out with one of the young housemen, Joel Masters, quite a bit, don't you?'

'Yes. I go out with other people too.'

He regarded her searchingly. 'He's not your type.'

Kym was astonished, and also a little annoyed. 'Why not?'

Harley shrugged. 'He's conceited, inclined to be insubordinate, a bit superficial I fear. Also, he's too young for you. You need an older man!'

'Well, I like him,' said Kym. 'He's fun.' She knew Harley and Joel did not like each other professionally. There had been, she felt sure, a serious clash of personalities at some time.

Harley said slowly, 'Is that all you want, fun?'

She met his gaze levelly. 'It's all you want, isn't it?'

He did not answer but said, 'I was surprised when I learned you had married so young. You always said you wanted to have a career. But you gave up nursing . . .'

Kym averted her eyes. 'I guess I changed my mind.'

'Must have been someone very special to change it,' he suggested.

She was careful how she worded her reply. 'Life is full of unexpected happenings. It doesn't always turn out the way we plan.'

He laughed. 'Like falling in love. I guess it's changed the course of a good many people's lives, even made them alter their priorities.'

'Not you, though,' Kym said, 'you've never been in love?'

'I think I might have been once, but I told you, I lost her. 'A shadow crossed his face, and Kym felt he was probably speaking the truth.

'Her fault or yours?' she ventured.

'She wasn't in love with me,' he said resignedly.

'It was probably just as well,' said Kym. 'You could never remain faithful to one woman, could you?'

He looked stung. 'You say some quite nasty things to me! I believe I could be utterly faithful to the woman I loved enough to marry.'

Kym burst out laughing. 'But you won't take the risk of marrying, Harley, I'm quite sure.'

'I'm getting too set in my bachelor ways. Nobody will have me!'

'Lucinda Raymond might,' Kym said slyly.

His eyebrows rose. 'You seem to know more about it than I do!' He spoke lightly but she detected a slight uneasiness in his tone and knew she had touched on a delicate topic.

'Try asking her,' she said.

He chuckled softly. 'Maybe I will!'

'I don't suppose she would be too happy if she knew you were out with me tonight,' Kym said.

'She's not being deprived,' he said slowly, 'she's in America until October.'

Kym drew a sharp breath. So that was why he suddenly had the time and inclination to chase around after her. Lucinda was abroad and Harley was at a loose end. And seven years ago she had been one of his conquests. No doubt he thought she would easily be again.

He was saying, 'And you, would you marry again?'

'Only if I met someone I could love.'

'Simon needs a father,' he commented, echoing her mother.

'I know,' Kym said, 'but I couldn't marry anyone just to provide him with a father.' She added practically, 'Marriage lasts longer than active fatherhood.'

Harley seemed to find the remark amusing. 'And you'd be stuck with him for the rest of your life. Yes, I see your point.'

'I think it's time we discussed something less personal,' Kym said firmly, feeling that the conversation was beginning to get too involved.

To her relief Harley took her up on it and plunged into a discussion on medical ethics which absorbed them both for the remainder of the evening, until it was time to leave.

Harley drove back to London in comparative silence, and Kym found that she suddenly had little to say. There was a tension between them, perhaps because they had disagreed slightly on one topic, but she sensed that it was also something more subtle than that.

They were still some miles from London when Harley suddenly pulled off the road into a layby and stopped the car. Kym automatically moved further away from him, facing him with her blue eyes flashing accusingly.

'You promised . . .' she said through gritted teeth.

His hand rested on her knee. 'I know, and I don't break promises, but I might not be able to help myself if you don't at least let me kiss you.' He slid strong arms around her and drew her close. Kym felt a warmth stealing over her as his lips touched hers, and it was like being filled to overflowing with warmth, as though before she had been a hollow shell, and now feeling was flowing back into her, filling her right up until she could hold no more. She felt her arms rise involuntarily to clasp him to her, and in his arms she was as malleable as a sponge.

'Kym . . .' The intensity of his voice as well as his body told her how much he desired her. He buried his face in her neck, kissing her fervently, his lips searing her skin, and sending waves of pleasure through her whole body. Suddenly she didn't care about promises, she wanted him as much as he wanted her.

'Kym . . .' He sensed the change in her, her responsive need, and raised his lips from hers to look into her face. 'Kym, darling, you torment me beyond endurance. I want you . . .'

His hands were seeking urgently under her sweater, and the warm skin of her midriff thrilled to the sudden hard contact of his fingers, telling her she wanted more . . . But this searing reminder of how much she wanted him also served to ring warning bells in her head, and with a stupendous effort, she reluctantly withdrew from his embrace.

'You promised . . .' she whispered hoarsely.

He almost shook her in his frustration. 'I know, but you can release me from it. You want to make love, you know you do . . .'

'No, Harley, please, there's no point . . .'

'Point! What in heaven's name is the point if it isn't that here and now we are both so consumed with desire for each other, we're just torturing ourselves denying it?'

Kym sighed deeply. 'Oh, it's always so simple for a man . . .'

He clenched his teeth and said huskily, 'Do you think it's easy for me to sit here arguing with you when all I want to do is . . .'

'Don't say it!' she begged. 'Let's go home, Harley. I realise I shouldn't have come out with you. I should have known it would end like this.'

He touched her face with lightly stroking fingers. 'Kym, come back to my place. Please . . .'

She steeled herself. 'No, Harley, I've already said no.'

His fingers cupped her chin and he drifted a light kiss over her lips, making her shudder with a new shaft of desire. He was experienced in the art of seduction, there was no doubt of that. He knew that small tantalising gestures could be as arousing as more obvious passion.

'Tell me,' he said softly, with an insidious persuasiveness, 'what is wrong with two adult people making love if they both want to?'

'Everything—if they're not in love,' Kym said bleakly. She added defensively, 'Maybe that's old-fashioned and unsophisticated, but it's the way I feel.'

He gripped her chin now, pinching it between thumb and forefinger, and said thickly, with a penetrating gaze, 'You made love to me once when you weren't in love with me.'

She flashed back instantly, 'And I've regretted it ever since!'

The force of her words made him retreat, taking his hands from her. She covered her face with her own hands, feeling desperately weary of the whole argument. She wanted to fall into his arms, to go back to his house with him, and the feeling that she didn't care what happened so long as she lay in his arms, was growing almost too strong for her to bear.

'Why?' he asked in a low voice.

Kym looked at him as she dragged her hands down from concealing her face. She could not tell him that she had been in love with him even then, and that she wouldn't have made love to him otherwise. She said, 'I was young and foolish then. I'm older and I hope a little wiser now.'

'You're incomprehensible!' he exclaimed impatiently.

'Are you going to take me home now?' she asked.

He grasped the steering wheel so tightly the skin was taut over the bones in his fingers, and his mouth was set. 'I suppose I might as well. You've made me feel a bit of a heel. And a fool to boot!'

Kym relaxed a little. 'There's no reason why you should feel like that.'

'No, perhaps not . . .' he said, in a rather enigmatic tone.

They drove the rest of the way in total silence. It was very late and for that as well as other reasons, Kym did not ask him in for coffee. He did not seem to be expecting it anyway. They said a rather cool goodnight, and Harley did not touch her.

On Monday Kym was shifted from Wren to Mildred ward, a women's surgical ward where there had been a rash of emergencies. As the load was lighter on Wren at the moment, Sister Muir had suggested she might like to get some further experience. Kym was grateful, particularly as it meant she would probably see less of Harley. She assumed that what had happened between them on Saturday night would mean the end of their association outside the hospital. However, there was still the following Saturday's date looming on the horizon. Kym decided he simply would not turn up, but she was half afraid that if she told Simon he would not be coming, he might just arrive to keep his promise to the boy, and then she would look foolish. So, in order that there should be no mistake about it, she decided she would have to see him.

A couple of days later, she went along to his office at a time she knew he was most likely to be there. He answered her knock with a brisk, 'Come in!' and seemed surprised when he saw who it was.

'Kym!' A smile broke briefly across his features, his eyes held hers.

'I won't keep you more than a minute . . .' she

faltered, her composure ruined by the impact of his devastating presence. She had not seen him for three days, and this, alarmingly, only seemed to have heightened her reaction to him.

He motioned her to a chair. 'Sit down.' There was a slight pause. 'I've been meaning to have a word with you, to apologise for the other night. I was brash and unfeeling and I don't blame you for being thoroughly disgusted with me.'

An apology was the last thing Kym had expected. 'Don't apologise, Harley, please,' she said, 'because I was partly to blame. I should not have let it reach the point . . . that it did. But I didn't come to talk about that, it's all forgotten. We were both rather silly.'

He eyed her doubtfully. 'You've transferred to Mildred ward,' he accused. 'Because you know it's off my beat?'

'I didn't know,' she said innocently. 'Anyway, it was Sister Muir's idea. They're chock-a-block down there and we were light on. She thought the experience would be good for me.'

He looked as though he only half believed her. 'I see. I thought perhaps you were afraid I might pounce on you in the ward.' Faint sarcasm edged his tone.

Kym forced a light retort. 'Would you have?'

His lips curved in amusement. 'Only my innate sense of protocol and fear of Gremlin reprisals would have stopped me!'

Kym supposed it was good that, in spite of everything, they could banter about it, but it wasn't getting to the point of her visit, so she went on, 'I just came to say that it would be better if you didn't come on Saturday. I'll explain to Simon that you're busy, and I'll take him anyway, so he won't be disappointed.'

His expression hardened, and he came around to her side of the desk and sat on the edge of it near her. He examined her carefully with his eyes, and she felt her skin tingle all over, as though a glance were a caress.

'In other words,' he said in a carefully controlled voice, 'you are giving me the brush off—again?'

Kym flinched at the reference to the time seven years ago she had discontinued their relationship. 'If you want to put it like that,' she answered evenly, struggling to keep her voice calm and her nerves steady. She laced her fingers tightly together to keep them from trembling.

His eyes never left her face. He seemed to be trying to see right inside her head. Then the hardness in his eyes vanished and was replaced by a softer look, a look that had the power to change her from being firm into utterly vulnerable.

'I know I blotted my copybook like some callow youth,' Harley said in a cajoling tone, 'but I promise I won't do it again.'

Kym drew in a deep breath and steeled herself to resist him. 'Your promises are empty,' she said flatly, 'You can't keep them. The answer is still the same.'

The contrition in his eyes was almost irresistible when he pleaded, 'Kym, why?'

She shook her head. 'I've just told you why! Do we have to go over it all again?'

'I'm not so sure we already have,' he answered reflectively. 'You haven't entirely satisfied me with your enigmatic and evasive answers. Why can't we take up where we left off?'

Kym screwed her hands together. 'Because we can't, that's why. I told you I don't want a casual affair with you.'

'All right, we won't have an affair,' he said generously. 'It'll be hard, but if that's the way you want it, I'll do my best to behave.'

Kym could not understand his persistence, unless it was simply that he saw her as a challenge, and her resistance as a threat to his ego. She said pointedly,

'There are plenty of other girls you can fill in time with until Lucinda gets back.'

He folded his arms across his chest. 'You have a pretty low opinion of me, haven't you? Based on what? Hospital gossip? I'd have believed better of you, Kym. Are you sure you're being fair?'

'Cautious, Harley,' she replied. 'I can't trust you, can I?'

He pursed his lips, biting back words of exasperation, she felt sure. A rueful grin parted his lips. 'That's your fault for being so damned desirable!'

She shrugged. 'There really isn't any point in discussing it, Harley.'

'You definitely don't want to see me again . . . outside the hospital?'

'I think it would be wise.' Kym stood up. She had made herself quite clear, and now she just wanted to escape from his disturbing presence.

She was trembling inside from tension and she swayed slightly as she pushed back the chair. Standing, she was very close to him where he half leaned against, half sat on the edge of the desk. He reached out a hand to steady her, and the touch electrified them both. In a moment she was in his arms, his mouth was crushing hers, and all she had said was wiped out under the onslaught of a wild passion that overwhelmed them both with its spontaneous intensity. She had responded before she could stop herself, and in a sudden flood of love and desire she was clinging to him desperately. How long they were locked together in each others' arms she did not know. Fortunately no-one came in or they might have been rather startled to see a staff nurse in the arms of a consultant.

At last Harley let her go. 'Now tell me why we shouldn't be lovers?' he said huskily.

There was a note of triumph in his voice, and it instantly kindled her anger.

'Because that's all you want,' she hurled at him. 'Lovers! Anyone who takes your fancy must end up your lover. But not me, not again. I'll never make that mistake again . . .' She turned away, dry-eyed, shaking. She had almost said too much.

He caught her shoulders and turned her to face him. 'Mistake? You weren't in love with me, you said so yourself, so how was it a mistake?' He seemed genuinely perplexed.

The urge to tell him, to drop her bombshell and shock him as he had doubtless never been shocked before, was almost overpowering, but with an effort of will she conquered it.

'I think I'd better go now,' she said, quaveringly. 'I've been absent from the ward rather a long time, and Sister only gave me permission for a few minutes . . .'

He would not let her go yet. 'Kym,' he said softly. 'Is there something I don't understand, something you ought to explain to me better than you have done? You haven't convinced me with what you've said so far.'

Kym shook her head wearily. 'Please, just leave me alone. There's nothing to explain. I don't want an affair with you and that's all there is to it.'

His hands dropped to his sides, and she left the room without looking at him again.

That night she went out with Joel but she felt edgy and unhappy, and did not really enjoy the evening. Harley was on her mind the whole time, spoiling it for her.

It was Friday before she saw Harley again, and this time he summoned her to his office. His voice sounded muffled when he called to her to come in, and she found him standing with his back to her, facing the window that looked out over the river. It was almost like a continuation of their previous conversation except that she had come at his request this time.

'Harley . . . you wanted to see me?' she asked tentatively, feeling distinctly uneasy.

He turned around and his face wore a grim expression. The lines in it seemed more sharply drawn than before, and Kym wondered what had happened and how it concerned her. It was plain that Harley was deeply troubled, and also angry.

He smiled, but it was a thin meaningless parting of his lips. He crossed to his desk and picked up an envelope, tipping out of it a handful of photographs. Kym saw that they were the ones Simon had taken at the zoo.

'Oh, you've had them developed already,' she said, going closer to look at them.

'Yes. Simon took some very good ones of the animals,' Harley said, displaying the prints for her on the desk top. 'Also a good one of you and me, and this is quite nice that I took of you two.' He spoke normally enough, but it seemed to Kym he was holding himself in check, for what reason she could not guess.

'Wasn't there one of the three of us?' she asked. 'Didn't it come out?'

He was, she realised, holding one print in his hand. He placed it in front of her. 'Here it is. Very good, don't you think?'

Kym looked at the print. It was very good of all three of them. But it made her want to weep. Harley, Simon and her, together—arms around each other—all smiling happily . . .

'Yes,' she agreed, 'it's very good. Simon will be pleased with his efforts. You must let me pay . . .'

'Kym!' His voice was quivering with suppressed anger. His control was slipping.

She stepped back, startled, and looked at him in alarm. His eyes burned into hers accusingly, and then his voice seemed to fill the whole room. He did not speak loudly, but there was a frightening intensity of emotion in his words.

'He's mine, isn't he? Simon is my son.'

Kym closed her eyes. She felt ready to crumple into a

heap at his feet. He knew! And she realised instantly how he knew. He might never have recognised himself in the boy, in the flesh, but the photograph showed a startling likeness and he had noticed it. She stared at the print helplessly, unable to speak.

When she did not answer he went on, 'I thought there was something odd about it all. You told me Simon was going on for six, but he happened to let slip he'd had his sixth birthday some time ago. I wondered if you were hiding something but it wasn't my place to pry. I just assumed you must have been pregnant when you married. I didn't do any careful adding up. But the last time you were here in my office I think I began to suspect the real truth. When I collected these photographs yesterday it didn't strike me at first, but I kept looking at that one for some reason, and eventually it dawned on me.' His eyes were piercing, daring her to challenge the truth. 'It is true, isn't it?'

Kym sank into a chair. 'Yes . . . yes, it's true.' It seemed as though a great burden had been lifted from her shoulders, but she knew the relief would only be temporary. The new burden she might have to bear could be greater.

'Why didn't you tell me?' he demanded.

She locked her fingers together to stop them shaking. 'I . . . I couldn't . . . not after what you'd said about your career, not settling down. I just couldn't. You might have felt obliged to marry me and I knew that wasn't the kind of marriage I wanted either. It would never have lasted.'

'So you went to Australia and concocted this story of being a widow?'

'It was easier that way. I didn't mind being an unmarried mother, but my mother did, so I changed my name by deed poll.'

'And there never was a Mr Rutherford?'

She shook her head. 'No.'

He began to pace the room. 'And all these years I've had a son . . .' He turned on her fiercely. 'I can't take it in . . . Simon is *my* son!'

Kym swallowed hard. 'Harley, I don't expect you to do anything about it. In fact I'm sorry I ever let myself be persuaded to come back to St A's. I shouldn't have done. It was bound to come out in the end, I suppose. But you see now why I couldn't . . . well, why . . .' Words utterly failed her.

'I don't see at all,' he said. 'But that doesn't matter. The point is that I have just discovered that I have a son.'

'I'm sorry, I never meant you to know—at least when I first came back I did decide to tell you, but I changed my mind . . .'

'Why?'

Kym shrugged. 'It would only complicate our lives. I don't want Simon to be a millstone around your neck. It's not your responsibility.'

'Like hell it's not! You let me find out I have a son and then say it's not my responsibility.'

'I wish you hadn't found out,' Kym whispered.

There was a highly charged silence during which Harley stood with his hands behind his back staring at the white wall of his office and the garish modern painting that adorned it. Kym waited apprehensively. She was too stunned to be able to think clearly.

When he turned to face her again, his face was still grim. 'Well,' he said, 'what do we do now?'

Kym bit her lip, and managed to say in a small voice. 'I don't know. I don't want anything from you.'

He did not appear to hear her. 'I'll tell you what we are going to do,' he said, and coming over to her chair placed both his hands on the arms. His face loomed close to hers. His eyes were steely and determined, as he pronounced very clearly and deliberately, 'We are going to get married.'

CHAPTER SIX

HARLEY'S words echoed around the room, and in Kym's head. She put a hand to her forehead, unable to believe that she had heard him properly. Then she looked at him blankly. This was ridiculous; she knew he didn't want to marry her.

'No,' she said flatly.

He stood up, arms folded across his broad chest, chin jutting aggressively. 'What do you mean, no?'

'I mean no we do not have to get married.' If only he knew how much she wanted to marry him, Kym thought desperately.

Harley's voice was low, his words clipped, 'You're perfectly correct, of course. There is no law that insists we marry because we have produced a child, but it would seem reasonable to want to legitimise the situation.'

'So far as anyone else knows it is perfectly legitimate,' Kym said.

'But you know it isn't, I know it isn't, and your mother knows. One day Simon will have to know. What is he going to think of your deception? Don't you think he would like to have a legitimate father?'

Kym bit her lip. What Simon might say when he learned the truth was a thought she had often entertained and then put purposefully away, not wanting to think about it. But one day he would need to see his birth certificate, and then she would have to tell him the truth, or let him think badly of her. Would he believe she had just refused to name his father, or would he wonder if she simply didn't know who it was? If she married Harley there would be no problem. But Harley didn't want to marry her.

'You don't really want to marry me,' she said. 'You're over-reacting, that's all.'

He laughed harshly. 'What do you expect? It isn't every day a man discovers he has fathered a son!' He bent towards her again. 'Is battling on alone a sensible alternative?'

Kym shook her head agitatedly. 'I can't marry you, Harley . . .' Her troubled blue eyes appealed to him. 'Nothing's changed . . .'

'Not even for Simon's sake?' he said cruelly.

The barb slid home painfully. It was so plain now why he had asked her. 'That's all you care about, isn't it? That you have a son!'

His eyes flashed dangerously. 'I most certainly do care about it. And I'm angry because you saw fit not to tell me in the first place.' His features were grimly set, and she suspected that whatever he felt for her physically was fast fading as a result of this startling development.

She said coldly, 'I wonder if you would have been quite so thrilled seven years ago!'

'How the hell would I know how I'd have felt? You didn't even give me a chance to find out!'

She matched his anger with a counter-attack. 'No, because I didn't want to be humiliated! I didn't want to be a drag on you, resented for the rest of my life because of a silly mistake!' She could have added that having broken off their relationship she could hardly have turned round and expected him to marry her.

'My mistake as well as yours!' he reminded her.

'Oh, you can be all noble about it now,' Kym said bitterly, 'but if you'd married me then because you felt obliged to we'd have been bickering worse than this in the first five minutes. You'd have resented me . . .'

'Wouldn't *you* have resented me?' he countered. 'After all, I got you into the mess.'

There was no point in denying it. If he guessed that all the time she had loved him, he might use it as a lever to persuade her to marry him now, and Kym was determined not to be persuaded. She would never marry a man, not even the father of her son, if he did not love her. She had made up her mind about that seven years ago and it had not changed.

'What sort of life would it have been for Simon?' she demanded. 'And how do you think I'd have felt, knowing you were seeing other women?'

'You really do have a low opinion of me, don't you?' He retreated a step, regarding her with a bleak expression. 'You don't know that it would have been so.'

'Please, Harley, don't try to whitewash the truth,' Kym begged wearily. 'You had other girlfriends all the time you were taking me out.'

'Didn't you have other boyfriends?' he countered.

'Yes . . .'

'Well, then . . .'

Their eyes were locked on this impasse. Kym sighed impatiently. 'That's just it! We went to bed together. We weren't in love. It was just . . . a physical thing.'

'Which is still there,' he insisted quietly. 'You can't deny that, Kym.'

'It isn't the basis for a marriage,' she maintained stubbornly.

'It could be a start.'

She looked at him and knew that his feelings towards her in that way had not changed after all. She drew in a long, deep breath. It could be . . . or it could lead her into even greater hurt than she was suffering now. She held on to her resolve. 'It wouldn't work, Harley, and you know it. You wouldn't be asking me to marry you now if it weren't for Simon. The thought would never have crossed your mind. I'm not the kind of woman you will marry—if you ever do, that is, which I strongly doubt. I'm a nurse and you're a consultant. You'll marry someone in your own sphere, or someone like . . . Lucinda Raymond . . . not a staff nurse!'

'So I'm a snob as well, am I?'

'I didn't say that! I'm just being factual. You're shock-ed because you've found out you have a son. Your conscience has been stirred, but when you take time to think it over, you'll realise how disastrous our marriage would be. It would only be a marriage of convenience—or rather inconvenience to you. We belong to different worlds now.'

'So what am I to do, send a monthly cheque?' he asked with a sneering twist to his mouth.

Kym bridled. 'I never wanted to ask you for money, or put you in the position where you felt obliged to offer it. I wouldn't want Simon or myself to be a millstone around anyone's neck.'

'I might want a say in my son's upbringing.'

Kym pursed her lips. 'I suppose I can't deny you that now.'

He turned abruptly away from her again, and his whole body was tense. She tried to understand how he was feeling. Harley was the kind of man who liked and usually got his own way. He had made up his mind, impetuously perhaps, but he had made it up nonethe-less, to do the right thing and marry her, but he hadn't bargained on her refusal. His whole attitude showed he did not like being thwarted, and she had a feeling he would not give up easily.

When he turned to face her again, he was still tense, but smiling. 'Kym,' his voice was even mildly cajoling. 'This has been one hell of a shock. I never dreamed . . . I can't quite believe it even now. We're both a bit strung up about it, naturally, so can I ask you, please, to go away and think about what I've said. Think very careful-ly about it, and don't make a hasty decision.' He came back to her and reached for her hands which were ice cold, and began to warm them between his own. 'I understand that from your point of view you feel it would be a travesty of a marriage, and that it would end your chances of happiness of the kind you hope for, but think of Simon.' He gave her a long considering look. 'Simon would have his rightful name. And . . . well, we could always amicably divorce eventually, if you wished it.'

Kym smiled wryly. 'Yes, I suppose that would be a handy solution.'

'I'm just asking you to think about it,' he repeated quietly. 'I'll see you and Simon next Saturday, not tomorrow, but a week tomorrow. You can give me your answer then.'

'Harley, I . . .' she began, but he drew her to her feet, still holding her hands, and refused to listen.

'Kym, please do as I ask. Please think about it.' He let go of her abruptly and turned to the desk, scooping up the photographs. 'Here, you'd better take these for Simon.' He held up the one of the three of them together, a rueful twist to his lips. 'This one, I think I'd better keep for the time being.' He thrust the others into her hands. 'You can tell Simon I'm tied up tomorrow, but I'll be there next Saturday for sure.'

There was a knock at the door and one of the registrars looked in to see if Harley was free. Since there was no point in further protest at that point, Kym left. She went back to the ward in a daze. Everything was now in a worse mess than before, and her emotions more confused than ever. She had never dreamed that he would offer to marry her now. She had not bargained on this reaction to his learning that Simon was his son.

His only thought was for Simon, and she had to give him some credit for that, she thought. She wondered if he would have felt the same way if he had not yet met Simon. They had got along so well together, it was really no wonder he felt proprietary about the boy. But surely he was the one to do the thinking. And doubtless he would. When he cooled down and took a rational view of things he would probably regret his rash proposal, and more than likely on Saturday week he would tell her so.

Whatever he said, she would remain firm in her resolve not to marry him. He did not want her, he wanted Simon. Oh, he might want to go to bed with her, but that was as far as it went. The fact that he had even mentioned divorce as an eventual way out for both of them showed he had considered their marriage a mere temporary device. He wanted to give Simon his name, and then what happened after that was not too important. Kym knew that if she married him she would end up sharing his bed, and then she would hate herself. And when the break-up came, as it inevitably would, she would be more heartbroken than ever. Was it really necessary to make so big a sacrifice for Simon?

'I'll tell Simon the truth one day,' she kept consoling herself. 'He'll understand. Surely he will? He wouldn't want me to have endured a sham marriage just to give him a name. Illegitimacy is nothing to be ashamed of. He won't hold it against me when he knows why I couldn't do it.'

But there were always lingering doubts deep inside her, however finally she thought she had convinced herself. Harley was prepared, apparently, to turn his life upside down for the boy, while she, Simon's own mother, was not. Harley would lose Lucinda if he married her. She would lose nothing—except, she thought bleakly, her self respect.

The following week seemed interminable. Kym tossed and turned nightly, miserable and uncertain, dreading the Saturday outing. Sometimes she wished she had never been born. Sometimes she even planned to run away with Simon, back to Australia, certain that Harley would lose interest if they were out of the country. She was sure he could not stop her going, nor force her to come back. But there was an obstacle to this plan. She knew her mother would not be happy there, but that she would go if Kym wanted her to. Kym refused to contemplate making such a demand on her. And she could not abandon her mother, since her mother had never abandoned her.

There was only one sensible solution, and she intended to put it to Harley. She would let him see Simon as often as he wished. She would let him have a say in the child's upbringing and education, and she would have to accept gratefully any support he felt inclined to offer. She felt sure he would see this as an acceptable alternative to a marriage he could not possibly want.

That this would cause her continual heartache, was something she would have to bear. It would not be easy seeing Harley frequently on home ground, hearing Simon calling him 'uncle', and she would suffer when he left to go to the arms of another woman.

Harley, of course, might soon tire of being a part-time father, which would be better for her, but possibly upsetting for Simon, since the boy showed every sign of becoming very attached to his 'uncle'. And if Harley married Lucinda, or anyone else, what might his wife have to say about it all? Or would he not tell her? Maybe he would never marry. Kym sighed over the possibilities many times. A whole Pandora's box of problems seemed to have been opened by her rash action in returning to St Alphage's.

When Saturday came, Kym tried to behave as though nothing untoward had occurred. Harley called for her and Simon as he had on the previous occasion, and they spent the whole day together. Most of the time was taken up with visiting Madame Tussaud's and the Planetarium, and having lunch in an Italian restaurant, which was Simon's choice.

Harley did not breathe a word on the subject of marriage, but it hovered between them like an unexploded bomb. And it only made matters worse for Kym seeing him playing the role of father as though born to it. There was, she noticed, a subtle difference in his attitude, a much more proprietorial air over Simon, and she surprised herself more than once by feeling just a shade jealous. Several times when father and son were engaged in whispered conversations, she felt left out.

And that's how it would be, she thought, if I married Harley. He would dote on Simon, be everything a father should be, but I should be just an appendage, an indispensable but not particularly wanted piece of a package deal. And suddenly the dreadful thought occurred to her, if Harley could have Simon without her he would undoubtedly do so. But that surely wasn't possible? She would never part with Simon, she vowed, whatever Harley did.

At the end of the day, when they finally got back to the flat, Harley said peremptorily, 'You're dining at my place tonight.'

Kym looked startled. 'Am I?' She bristled a bit. 'Since when have you had the right to order me around?'

'We can't talk at your place, or in public,' he insisted in a low voice. Then he flashed her one of his irresistible smiles. 'Mrs White promised to leave a sumptuous spread for you to heat up. She'll never speak to me again if she finds it still in the refrigerator.'

Kym did not want to go to his house, much less play housewife in his kitchen, but she really had no option. He had organised it so that they would be alone, in private, to talk, and she could hardly refuse to talk to him; this thing had to be settled, and the sooner the better. Reluctantly, she agreed to go with him.

All the way she tried not to think about it, just to watch the rear lights of cars streaming along beside them, and the headlights travelling in the opposite direction, until the kaleidoscope of traffic and traffic lights, the lights in buildings, the street lamps and reflections as the road became wet in a drizzling rain, seemed to hypnotise her. Harley did not speak, and the silence between them filled the car like a brooding monster.

He swung wide into Lowther Square, and Kym was momentarily flung against him. She drew away as though stung, yet conscious of the devastating effect even the least contact with him could have on her. That coming to Lowther Square with him was dangerous she was fully aware, and she knew she would have to be on her guard, not so much against him, as against herself.

There were lights on downstairs in the house, soft lighting in the hallway and drawing room. An intimate romantic atmosphere, Kym thought. It was an inviting house that seemed to close around you comfortably when you entered it, like an embrace. Kai, the Siamese, leapt onto the hall table, curled his tail around a vase of roses whose perfume wafted sensuously on the air, and mewed in the plaintive way of his species.

Harley rubbed the cat's head. 'Hello, Kai.' He turned to smile at Kym. 'Mrs White will have fed him but he'll cadge for more. Come on, I'll show you the kitchen.' There was a trace of the autocratic Dr Garfield in his tone.

'I know where the kitchen is,' Kym said stiffly.

'I'd better show you where to find an apron,' Harley said, unrebuffed.

'I expect Mrs White keeps hers behind the door, like most people,' said Kym airily, and marched out to the kitchen, the cat following on her heels.

Harley's quiet laughter also followed her, and his remark: 'Kai knows a sucker when he sees one!'

Did Harley think he could make a sucker of her, too?

Kym tossed her handbag onto a chair and surveyed the kitchen. She found a sheet of notepaper on the brown-tiled work bench with, as she expected, explicit instructions from Mrs White concerning what to do with the foil covered dishes she would find in the refrigerator, and the saucepans on the stove. Kym fetched the casserole and fruit pie from the refrigerator, then looked into the saucepans. One contained fresh broccoli, the other a creamy sauce waiting to be gently heated. Mrs White's instructions were brief and to the point. And the cream for the pie, she stated, was already whipped and in a bowl in the fridge.

Kym was just giving Kai a saucer of milk to stop him winding his lithe body in and out between her legs and mewing, when Harley strolled in.

'Everything all right?'

'Fine. All I have to do is turn the oven on and time it. Your housekeeper has prepared it all.'

He smiled with satisfaction. 'I told her you were very domesticated, but I didn't think I ought to test your culinary skills just yet.' It was the first indication he had given all day that he had not changed his mind, and Kym tensed as she realised it. Was it possible that he was not going to act in character after all?

'Harley . . . I . . .' she began falteringly.

'Not now,' he said firmly. 'We can discuss important issues later. I don't want my dinner spoilt. I'm very particular about food. I was just wondering what you would like to drink with dinner—red or white wine?'

'I really don't mind,' Kym said, wishing he would go away and stop making me feel apprehensive.

'Come and join me in the drawing room,' he invited. 'Things can take care of themselves for half an hour, can't they, while we have an aperitif?'

'Yes, I suppose so.' She waited until he had gone, then slowly followed, trying to give herself time to compose herself.

Seated on the big comfortably cushioned couch with a dry sherry to sustain her, Kym felt a little more in command of the situation, and herself. She knew now that Harley was going to try and change her mind, but she was determined not to weaken.

'I can see you haven't changed your mind,' he said at last, after studying her for some moments as he swirled whisky around in his glass.

'You're very perceptive,' she observed drily.

'It was written all over you all day,' he replied, equally as drily.

'Then I'm glad the message was clear without my having to spell it out.'

Harley swallowed a mouthful of the spirit. 'Simon is a real credit to you.'

'Thank you.' Kym accepted the compliment gracefully.

'We get along rather well, don't you think?'

'You and Simon? Yes, you seem to.'

He was smiling in a bemused sort of way. 'Funny, really. I took to that kid right from the start, before I knew. Blood will out, I suppose.'

'I suppose so.'

He eyed her steadily. 'Actually, I meant that we *all* get along rather well—all three of us. It was an enjoyable day wasn't it?'

'If you say so.' She met his gaze full on. 'Do I infer from that, that you haven't changed *your* mind?'

He regarded her contemplatively, and just having him looking at her made her heart race. Finally he said, 'I still want you to marry me.'

Kym stood up and placed her glass on the table. 'You know my answer,' she said, then, 'I'd better take a look in the oven.'

She escaped thankfully and managed to busy herself in the kitchen until the meal was ready to dish up. Harley did not intrude, and after a few moments she heard strains of piano music coming from the living room. She had not realised he played.

He was still playing when she went to call him. He did not hear or see her because he was half turned away from the door. She stood for a moment in the doorway thinking that this was how it could be, her and Simon and Harley, together in this beautiful house, everything they needed . . . Then she pulled herself up sharply. It was despicable to be tempted like that. Material gains could never make up for the heartache she would surely suffer in the end if she accepted Harley's convenient proposal.

'Dinner's ready,' she said, and instantly he stopped playing.

Mrs White had laid the table in the dining room, a room Kym had not seen before. It was as beautifully appointed as the other rooms in the house. 'I didn't know you were musical,' she commented as Harley poured the wine into sparkling crystal goblets.

He gave her an enigmatic half smile. 'My dear, there is a good deal you don't know about me.'

Kym retorted, 'Hardly surprising, since we haven't met for years.'

His glance now was mildly sardonic. 'Perhaps we ought to start getting to know each other better. You might even like me if you weren't so prejudiced.'

'Oh, I like you,' she rejoined airily.

'But you're in no danger of loving?'

'No danger,' she lied, averting her eyes. She didn't ask whether there was any danger of his falling in love with her. She knew there wasn't. Love might be an emotion Harley would learn to feel for his son—or was it only pride?—but loving a woman was not his way. Harley was self-contained, and, she felt sure, wanted to remain uncommitted emotionally. He would have fallen in love by now, she thought, if he was going to. He had admitted that he nearly had once, and the experience had evidently cured him of doing so again. He probably wasn't in love with Lucinda Raymond, she was merely a 'suitable wife' for him as someone had once said of her. Harley Garfield would never be a one-woman man.

He said directly, 'So you still refuse to marry me?'

'Yes.'

'Where do we go from here?' His voice had a steely edge.

Kym shrugged. 'I suppose that's up to you.'

'And you,' he added.

'What do you want to do?' she asked matter-of-factly, starting her meal with a nonchalance she did not feel. 'Mmm, this is very good. You are lucky to have Mrs White to look after you.'

'I'd rather have you!' The teasing look in his eyes faded as she met it with disdain. He went on matter-of-factly, 'I want to marry you, Kym. It's the tidiest solution, can't you see that?'

'Tidy!' She half choked on the exclamation.

'Perhaps a bad choice of word. I never was very good with words. Flowery phrases aren't my style. I just think it's the only feasible course for both of us. All the facts say so.'

'Do they?'

'I believe so. You said a few minutes ago that you liked me. That's a start because I . . . like you too. We are sexually compatible, we know that to be true . . .'

'I don't know how you can say . . .' she found herself floundering under the steely blue-grey gaze.

'Come, Kym, you know it's true. We strike enough sparks off each other to set the whole of London on fire!'

'That's an extravagant claim.'

'You know it's true.'

'Fires eventually burn themselves out,' Kym said.

He laughed softly. 'You know perfectly well I would only have to come around, take you in my arms and kiss you to prove my point.'

Her eyes flashed at him. 'Don't you dare!'

'There you are! You're scared to put it to the test.'

'All right, what else?' she said patiently.

'We have a great many interests in common besides our work. That's something we've discovered on the two outings we've had lately. Have we ever been short of a topic of conversation?'

'Your conversation has been a bit one track,' Kym said unfairly.

He laughed. 'You're a bit pert sometimes, but I guess I deserve the odd barbed remark. I predict we'd argue quite a bit, but a life without the spice of argument would be very dull indeed.'

'You're putting a watertight case. Anything else?'

'Your mother let slip that you're a very good cook, and I can see for myself that you'd be a perfect hostess.' He was openly mocking her now.

'You sound more like an employer than a prospective husband.'

'I shall ignore that. I know you are usually more witty than flip.'

'Harley, this conversation is a waste of time,' said Kym, growing impatient. 'Let's talk about practicalities. Like how often do you want to see Simon? We ought to make some arrangement to suit both our schedules. That is if you want to see him regularly.'

'It isn't what I want,' he said sharply. 'I don't want to be a part-time father. I want you and Simon here, in my house, my family.' His frustration at being unable to talk her round was showing in his tone of voice.

'*You* want—always what you want,' Kym said a trifle bitterly. 'So long as you get what you want it doesn't matter about anyone else, is that it?'

His impatience broke through. 'For heaven's sake, Kym, what's wrong with getting married? I can offer you a whole lot more than most men!'

'Now you're trying to bribe me!' she retorted hotly.

He ran his fingers through his hair. 'I'm not! We've got a whole lot more going for us, Kym, than most couples.'

'I think you are kidding yourself because you want Simon,' Kym said. 'And I wouldn't expect you to understand how I feel.' Love was an irrelevancy to him, she thought bitterly.

'I want my son to have his father's name,' Harley said, and all at once there was a dangerous glint in his eyes.

Kym noted it but kept cool. 'You want,' she echoed

derisively. 'There you go again. You only found out about Simon a week ago, and now you think you can call the tune.'

'It was hardly my fault I found out only a week ago!'

Kym bit her lip. She had erred in making that remark. 'All right,' she conceded, 'perhaps I should have told you in the beginning, but it doesn't alter the fact that I still believe an unborn baby would have been less attractive to you than a six-year-old who flatters your ego!'

He drew his lips together in a taut line. 'Well, you certainly don't!'

Kym rose and went out to the kitchen to fetch the raspberry pie. While she was serving it, Harley said in a quieter tone, 'There's someone else, isn't there? That's why you won't marry me. I know you can't still be in love with a husband who doesn't exist, so who is it? Are you in love with Joel Masters?'

'Joel and I are colleagues and friends,' Kym said, 'that's all.' She could not help, however, the slight colour that flowed into her cheeks, and knew that Harley noticed.

'But you think you might be falling in love with him?' he persisted.

Kym drew a deep breath as she handed him his plate, mechanically. It seemed incongruous somehow, combining the normality of eating a meal with emotional drama. Perhaps, she thought, it wouldn't hurt to let him think she was falling for Joel. 'I might be,' she said in a noncommittal tone that she saw instantly infuriated him.

Harley's eyes narrowed. 'Does he know about Simon?'

'Only as much as everyone else knows.'

'You'd have to tell him about me. He'd eventually become curious if I kept turning up to see Simon. He wouldn't swallow the uncle bit for long.'

'Harley, the question doesn't arise.'

'Yet.'

She shrugged. 'You're saying these things, not me. I'm not making any predictions. All I'm saying is that I don't want to marry you.' And it isn't true, she thought, I want to marry him more than anything else in the world.

'Because even if you're not in love with Joel, you think you might fall in love with someone else later. If that happened, Kym, I would let you go.'

She sighed, half smiling at him. 'And you—if you fall in love with someone else, I should have to let you go. Would you want that written into our marriage lines? No, Harley, I don't want a marriage on those sort of terms.'

He looked at her fully, and there was a veiled threat in the grey-blue eyes. 'I may not ask you again. I may not give you a second chance.'

'Is that a threat?'

'If you like.'

'It doesn't change my mind. I wish you would drop the subject, Harley, and talk about the situation as it now stands.' She began to collect the plates. 'Shall I bring the coffee into the drawing room?'

'Sure . . .' He spoke tersely, and got up from the table. 'Don't do any washing up. Mrs White doesn't like anyone else interfering with the dish-washer.'

He left her abruptly and Kym was glad of the short respite while she went to the kitchen alone and made the coffee. When she returned with it to the drawing room, Harley had put a music tape on and was leaning back in an armchair, eyes closed, hands clasped behind his head, looking as though he was asleep.

He leapt up, however, as she entered, and took the tray from her. The light brushing of his fingers against hers as he did so electrified her and she wondered dismally if there would ever come a time when he wouldn't affect her that way. He poured liqueurs while she sat on the couch and poured coffee for them both. He sat beside her and rested his hand on her knee. 'Tell me, Kym,' he began, then stopped and took his hand away.

'Tell you what?'

'Nothing. I was going to ask a very personal question, that's all.'

'You're suddenly very inhibited,' she commented, drily.

'You're beginning to inhibit me!' he admitted, with a slightly twisted grin. 'All right, I was going to inquire about your love life.'

Kym's face closed up. 'Well, that *was* rather a personal question.'

She placed her empty cup back on its saucer on the table. As she sat back, Harley moved closer, until his thigh touched hers. He slid his arm around her waist, pushing her back against the cushions and let his mouth drift across her lips, tantalisingly. He smiled teasingly into her eyes.

'You know you can't fight it, Kym.'

She struggled. 'I can and I will!'

'Why . . . ?' He held her fast, bending his head to her chest, and laughing softly. His warm breath fanned her tingling skin, arousing her almost as much as his kiss. What was it about this man that affected her so profoundly?

'Harley, we're not going to have an undignified struggle all over again, are we?' she pleaded.

He raised his head, smiling at her, that fleeting small-boy expression lurking in his face, the look she had sometimes glimpsed before and which could melt her heart as no other man's could do, the look that was so dangerous because it made her want to please him. It unleashed all the pent-up love she felt for him, and she knew that if she was not careful, sooner or later he would realise it and take advantage of it.

He shifted slightly, keeping his arm around her shoulders, pulling her head against his shoulder. His fingers

idly stroked her bare arm, a feather-like touch, and after
a minute or two of this soothing caress, Kym closed her
eyes, and lulled by the food and the wine, and the soft
music, she began to drift. Whether it was seconds or
minutes that she was asleep, she was unaware, but she
woke suddenly to find that his other hand had slipped
beneath her blouse and cupped one breast which he was
caressing with the same languorous sensuality as he had
her arm. Drowsily she looked up at him, aware only of
the waves of pleasure his touch was bringing to her, and
he bent his head to kiss her tenderly. She found herself
turning into his arms, drawing him down on top of her
with a little sigh of pleasure as she sank back against the
cushions piled at the end of the couch.

'Kym . . . darling . . .' His voice was a husky whisper
in her ear, as persuasive as his wandering hands were on
her body. The pressure of his hard muscular frame on
top of her slight one brought back a flood of memories of
that night seven years ago when she had so foolishly
succumbed to just the same kind of devilish seduction,
but only because she loved him and could not help
herself.

She tried to struggle now, but he took her faint
stirrings for response, and held her closer than ever, and
the deeper and more sensuous his kisses became, the less
resistance she was able to call up. A treacherous voice
dismissed her resolves and said she might as well marry
him. At least she would have him like this . . . sometimes. She would have his physical loving, a loving she
doubted she would find equalled in any other man. And
Simon would have a father. If she let him make love to
her now, she knew he would take her acquiescence as
the answer he wanted. But if she let him make love to her
it would be her undoing, another voice declared. She
would marry him because she would not be able to say
no.

He sensed her relaxing as she ceased to be able to fight

him either physically or mentally, and the voice of
reason was drowned out by the strength of desire. He
lifted his head, looking into her eyes with a faintly
triumphant tilt to his lips. Waves of longing washed over
her as his hands explored her trembling body, not
tentatively now, but with growing confidence because he
knew he had at last won the battle.

He kissed her again deeply and searchingly, and she
felt the rising urgency in him, and instinctively responded by moving her body questingly against his.
Then he parted his mouth from hers and shifted so that
his hands slid under her and he was able to lift her bodily
from the couch as he rose to his feet.

'Harley . . .' she whispered, but it was scarcely a
protest, more a sigh of surrender.

'We're going upstairs,' he murmured against her hair.

Every nerve strained towards wanting him. Her resistance had been banished beyond recall. But as he took
the first step towards the door there was an ear-splitting
sound, a duet of screams that filled the air for several
seconds. The sound seemed to come from the garden.

Kym was jerked out of her drowsy acquiescence, and
Harley, almost as startled, set her down on her feet.
There was a shared moment of wide-eyed alarm, and
Kym whispered fearfully, 'What on earth was that?'

And then Harley burst out laughing. 'Cats!' he exclaimed. 'Damn cats!'

Kym looked puzzled for a moment, then she too burst
out laughing as she recognised the sound, just as another
long caterwaul rent the silence.

Harley said wryly, 'The music of love!' He crossed to
the windows and flung them open. 'Get out of it!
Shoosh!'

As he shouted, Kai sidled in, blinking in the light, tail
held high, supercilious, and mewing plaintively.

Harley said, 'Kai is neutered, but he has a certain
curiosity about the love life of his neighbours. The toms

sometimes try to bash him up, but he's pretty good at holding his own.' He bent down and stroked the cat. 'You wicked old voyeur, you! I suppose you want a drink of milk now.'

'I'll get it,' said Kym, glad of something to do. She hurried out to the kitchen, straightening her clothes as she went. The cat stalked after her and Harley followed in their wake. Kym refilled the saucer on the kitchen floor, then glanced up at Harley who was watching her quizzically from the doorway.

'I'd better be going home,' she said, suddenly over-come with embarrassment.

He grasped her arm. 'Must you?'

But the intensity of the moment had passed. The interruption had broken the spell for them both. It would now be impossible to recapture the same mood, even if they wanted to. And Kym most certainly did not.

'Yes, please,' Kym said firmly, telling herself she ought to be eternally grateful for the rescue. She was appalled at her vulnerability, and the ease with which he had almost seduced her.

Harley knew he had no chance of regaining his advan-tage of earlier, so he smiled and said, 'Those damn cats have got something to answer for! Come on, then. I'll take you now.'

He drove fast and furious and, when they arrived at the flat, did not try to kiss her or even touch her. He said good night in an offhand way, and Kym left him quickly, knowing that whatever happened she must never be alone with him again.

CHAPTER SEVEN

KYM reluctantly faced up to the fact that although she might be scrupulously careful never to be alone with Harley, she had to accept that from now on—or for as long as he desired it—he was likely to be a part of her life, whether she wanted it or not. She had promised she would not deny him access to Simon, and having seen how wonderfully well the two got along together, she could not have denied Simon the chance to see him. Almost every other day Simon would ask, 'When's Uncle Harley coming again?'

And almost every week Harley announced some plan to take them somewhere. Kym always accompanied them, not because she did not trust Simon with Harley, but because it was always made extremely difficult for her not to go. Harley insisted, Simon insisted, and her mother urged her to go along with them. Sometimes Irene would be persuaded to go too, and with each succeeding weekend the illusion of a happy family outing grew, until Kym began to feel that the only reality was the time between her outings with Harley. With him she moved into fantasy land.

In spite of herself she began to relax. At first, after the near disastrous evening at his house, Kym had been very much on edge with him, but as time went on, she believed he had accepted the situation. He did not mention marriage again. It was possible, too, she reflected, that he was at last beginning to have second thoughts, and to realise what a mistake it would have been. Learning that he had a son had naturally turned his emotions inside out temporarily. Although, in a strange sort of way, Kym looked forward to their

outings, she always experienced a pang when she
was waiting for Harley to come, and seeing Simon
leap joyfully into his father's arms always caused her
pain.

The spontaneous affection that had sprung up between the man and boy did not wane, and it always
seemed to Kym that Harley genuinely enjoyed their
outings as much as Simon did. He always entered active-
ly into the spirit of things, taking Simon boating on the
Serpentine, helping him to put a kite together which
they flew with great gusto on Hampstead Heath, and
always letting Simon say what he would like to do.
Simon soon ran out of ideas but Harley never did.

Often, watching them together, engaged in some
boisterous outdoor activity, or heads together marvell-
ing over exhibits in the Natural History Museum, or one
of the transport museums which Simon adored, Kym
would shake her head in silent wonder. This was not the
autocratic Harley Garfield, consultant physician, nor
was it the Harley Garfield, playboy and confirmed
bachelor. He puzzled her greatly, and it was not until
they went one Saturday to the Tower of London, and
afterwards to look at the boats in St Katherine's Dock
nearby that she learned a little more about the enigma
that was Harley Garfield.

She and Harley were sitting in the sunshine enjoying a
drink, while Simon had for once pottered off on his own
to look at the vintage sailing ships and other nautical
curiosities moored in the nearby inlet.

'Don't you want to look around too?' Kym asked. 'I
don't mind. I'll sit here and rest for a while.'

Harley looked across at her, smiling. 'Simon's all right
poking about on his own. And I'm enjoying having you
to myself for a change.'

'You're very good to him,' Kym said slowly. 'I'm
afraid he's missed having someone to do things with.'

'I'm sure you've done your best.'

Kym sighed. 'I've tried. But I'm female, and boys like male company sometimes.'

'Boys need fathers,' Harley said, pointedly.

Kym wished the conversation had not taken this turn. It was her fault, of course. She tried to edge it away from dangerous ground by saying, 'Did you grow up in London?'

He stared into the distance beyond the buildings and the masts of the sleek white yachts moored nearby in the marina, and then said, 'No . . . I grew up in the north of England. My father was a miner. He left us when I was four, and my sister was a baby. We've never seen him since.'

'Oh . . . so you never really knew him.'

'No. I never had a father . . . that I can remember. There was no-one to take me to cricket matches or football, or to teach me to fly a kite, or hoist me on his shoulders and run helter-skelter downhill . . .'

Kym was deeply moved. It explained in part why he was so eager to do things with Simon. He was living now the childhood he had missed. And she saw too why he didn't want Simon to miss out. It had scarred him deeply not having a father.

He went on, 'My mother died when I was ten and my sister and I went to live with our maternal grandmother who had not approved of my mother's marriage. She was very strict and she did not really like small boys. She related much better to my sister. Nevertheless she was very fair and did all she could for both of us. For some reason Marianne and I both wanted to do medicine, and although Grandmother was a bit horrified at the idea of Marianne becoming a doctor she did not try to stop her. When she died she left us everything, the house and some investments to me, and an equal legacy to Marianne. The old girl was much wealthier than we had ever imagined. We're both very grateful to her.'

'But you always hankered for a father,' Kym said

slowly, not a little astonished by these revelations.

'I suppose I did.' His eyes met hers and she wondered suddenly if he would still marry her if she said she had changed her mind. He wanted Simon to have what he had not, and, initially at any rate, he had been prepared to make a sacrifice himself so that it should be so. He had earned her admiration for that.

Simon came running up to them, full of shining-eyed enthusiasm for what he'd seen. He perched on the bench beside Harley.

'I'm going to buy a big yacht and sail around the world,' he declared self-importantly.

Harley laughed. 'All by yourself?'

Simon considered briefly. 'No, you can come too, and Mummy can come and do the cooking!'

'Thank you,' said Kym, laughing. 'I do have my uses then?'

'A boy at school's daddy has a yacht,' Simon informed them enviously. He added, 'They're rich.'

'They must be,' said Kym.

'I expect we'd be rich if my daddy hadn't died,' said Simon. 'I bet we'd have a yacht too.'

Kym and Harley exchanged a brief, amused glance. 'I don't think so,' Kym said with a laugh.

Simon confronted Harley. 'Are you rich, Uncle Harley?'

Harley laughed. 'I get by!'

'Simon,' reproached Kym, 'you shouldn't ask people such personal questions.'

Simon ignored her. 'Why don't you buy a yacht?' he demanded guilelessly of Harley.

Harley nodded thoughtfully. 'Hmmm . . . it's not a bad idea. Maybe I will one of these days.'

Simon considered him with great seriousness for a moment, then startled them both by saying, with a beaming smile, 'I wish you were my daddy!'

Kym's heart flipped over and she did not dare look at

Harley, who coped expertly by saying, 'If I were your daddy I ought to tan your backside for being such an opportunist!'

Simon knew he was not serious. 'When you buy your yacht,' he said complacently, 'will you take Mummy and me with you?'

'Maybe . . . if you're both very good!' replied Harley, teasingly.

That outing left Kym in a depressed frame of mind. She had seen a facet of Harley she had not seen before, a part of him that perhaps explained his independent and uncommitted nature. She kept thinking of the small, emotionally deprived boy and feeling sorry for him. She also could not help thinking, again and again, that she was depriving Simon by not agreeing to marry Harley. And yet she could not wholly convince herself that in the long term it would be the right thing to do.

Harley's frequent visits were naturally commented on by Irene. At first she merely remarked that he was a nice man, and so good to Simon, and then she began to mention casually what a perfect little family party they made. Kym always shrugged off her remarks noncommittally, but she knew that sooner or later she was going to have to tell her mother the truth about Harley. Several times she almost did, but she knew that if Irene knew that Harley had offered to marry her, she would do her best to persuade her to change her mind. She would never believe, as Kym now did, that Harley had almost certainly changed his.

It intrigued Kym that her mother had never noticed the resemblance between Harley and Simon. Once Irene had remarked to Harley that Simon had his mother's nose and chin, but goodness knew where he got those charmer's eyes and that mischievous mouth from! Kym had caught her breath when Harley replied cheerfully, 'From his father, I expect!' His look for Kym had been full of silent laughter.

Kym was always a little afraid Harley would tell her mother the truth, knowing she would be on his side, but he did not. This led her eventually to believe that he had abandoned the idea of marriage at last.

She was getting ready to go out with Joel one evening, when her mother broached the subject of Harley.

'Do you think it's quite fair to Harley?' her mother asked, 'Going out with Joel behind his back?'

It was unlike her mother to voice even such a mild criticism. Kym turned around from the mirror where she was applying mascara to her long and very dark lashes. 'Harley is well aware I go out with Joel.'

'Yes, but Harley's obviously much fonder of you,' her mother said.

Kym shrugged. 'Not as fond as you think. His girl-friend is in America at the moment and I'm a handy substitute when he's at a loose end at weekends.'

Irene considered her daughter carefully. 'Simon thinks the world of him.'

'I know . . .'

'It would be so nice if . . .' her mother said hopefully.

'Mum,' interrupted Kym warningly, 'don't start jump-ing to conclusions. Harley finds Simon's adoration flattering. He'll soon get tired of it. When Lucinda comes back he'll be fully occupied and he won't have much time for us, I assure you.' She believed this to be true. She expected that Lucinda's reappearance would change Harley's attitude considerably. However, if he still wanted to see Simon regularly, that was the time she would tell her mother.

'Are you quite sure, Kym?' Mrs Andrews murmured reflectively. 'I've noticed the way he looks at you some-times . . .'

Kym darted her a sharp look. She must have noticed the sensuous glances that Harley sometimes directed at her, the small gestures like a hand on her shoulder, a swift straying of fingertips along her arm, a twirling of a strand of hair. She knew he did it on purpose to tantalise and annoy her, and also because he was the kind of person who couldn't help it. It meant no more than that the strong physical attraction between them was not dead, only being carefully kept in check. But Kym could not tell her mother that it was not fondness that made Harley appear affectionate.

She said lightly, 'Don't be fooled, Mum. I'm not! Harley is a flirt. He gets a kick out of touching hands, dropping a kiss here and there. It's just the way he is. The nurses think it's thrilling!'

'Well, I suppose you should know,' her mother conceded reluctantly.

'I know Harley better than you do,' Kym affirmed with a laugh. 'He has always been a flirt, and a confirmed bachelor. He'd have married long ago if he wasn't.'

'Did you know him before?' Irene asked, surprised. 'Was he at St Alphage's when you were there before?'

Kym could have kicked herself for giving that away. In a minute her mother was going to recall her saying she had gone out with him, and that might well lead to her discovering the truth. But now was not the moment to confess, so Kym drew a deep breath and, hoping her voice sounded as offhand as she was trying to make it, she said, 'Slightly. Mainly by reputation. He was a very junior houseman at St A's when I was there.'

Her mother seemed satisfied and did not pursue it. She said, with a touch of resentment, 'This Lucinda, who is she?'

'Lucinda Raymond? She's the daughter of the Chairman of the hospital board, and heir to a pharmaceutical fortune. A divorcee, very beautiful and glamorous, and Harley has been squiring her around for some time. Rumour has it that if he marries anyone he'll marry her. The grapevine says she's willing and obviously she's a highly desirable catch for anyone with ambitions in the medical world.'

'Unless he's not in love with her,' remarked Irene thoughtfully.

'That wouldn't stop Harley if she's got what he wants,' said Kym emphatically. After all, he had been prepared to marry her in order to get Simon.

'I don't know,' Irene said perplexed. 'You young people seem to be so sure of yourselves.' She added dubiously, 'You're not falling in love with Joel, are you?'

'Why? Don't you like Joel?' Kym was surprised. She had thought her mother was quite taken with him.

Irene said evasively, 'He's a very nice young man, but not . . . well, perhaps not quite steady enough for you and Simon.'

Kym gave a private laugh. 'And you think Harley would be?'

'Yes, I do.' Her mother was quite definite.

'Oh, Mum, you're on the wrong track. If anyone's unsteady, it's Harley. You've got your wires crossed, I'm afraid.'

Irene did not comment on that. 'Are you in love with Joel?'

'I don't know . . .' Kym hedged carefully. She had been asking herself that same question lately. If she could only relegate what she felt for Harley to some distant recess of her mind, and look at Joel without Harley's image spoiling everything, might she not find it within herself to love him? Carrying a torch for Harley was selfish, she had decided, and unfair to Simon. She must try and fall in love with someone who would love her.

She had begun to suspect that Joel might be that someone. In spite of all he had said at the beginning, lately he had begun to linger over a goodnight kiss, and Kym had sensed in him a seriousness that was new. He had mentioned married friends a few times recently with what had sounded suspiciously like envy. Kym sometimes tried to imagine what it would be like married to

Joel, but somehow could not form even a hazy picture of their life together. She was very apprehensive as to how he would take the truth about Simon. He and Harley did not get on well as she knew, and that could be a stumbling block.

Because of her mother's words, her own thoughts were more in the forefront of her mind that evening, so much so that at one stage Joel remarked on her air of preoccupation.

'You're a bit quiet tonight, Kym,' he said. 'Anything on your mind?'

She was startled out of a reverie. 'Oh, no . . . I'm sorry, I must have been drifting. What did you say?'

He smiled fondly at her. 'Nothing much. I was just looking at you, miles away, a rather sad expression in your eyes, almost as though you were remembering something that had hurt you deeply.'

'It was very rude of me,' she apologised.

'Was it . . . *him* you were thinking about?' Joel asked quietly.

'Him?'

'Simon's father. You still think a lot about him, don't you?' His tone was sympathetic but there was a tinge of jealousy lurking in it.

Kym tried to pass it off lightly. 'No, of course not, that was years ago.'

'But you still remember. I often notice it. You drift off suddenly into a sad sort of reverie.' He smiled regretfully. 'What chance does anyone else have while you're still in love with that man?'

She shrugged. 'I suppose you think I'm very foolish.'

He touched her hand tentatively. 'I think it's unfortunate. I shall never get to know you properly while you hanker for another man, even if he is dead.'

Kym forced a light tone. 'I thought you didn't want to get involved.'

His gaze was direct and very serious. He held her

fingers tightly and after giving her a long searching look, said slowly, 'I'm beginning to change my mind about marriage.'

She drew her hand away, laughing. 'You! I thought you were the bachelor type, half a dozen girls on a string, lots of fun and no responsibilities!'

He said seriously, 'That was before I started going out with you. I haven't taken another girl out for ages.'

'Which is a temporary state of affairs, I'm sure,' she countered.

'I'd like to make it permanent,' he said quickly, then went on, 'Kym . . . what would you say if I asked you to marry me?'

She hadn't expected it quite so soon. 'Joel, this is a bit sudden, isn't it? I thought you said you felt safe with me.'

'Very unsafe now,' he admitted, smiling rather sheepishly. 'I've got you under my skin, Kym. There's something about you that intrigues me, and I'm a bit tired of keeping you at arm's length, and being kept at arm's length myself. If you must know I think I've fallen in love with you.'

'What makes you think that?' she asked quietly.

'I saw you talking to Harley Garfield the other day. I know you go out with him sometimes . . .'

'How do you know that?' she broke in sharply, taken aback because she had not told Joel, or anyone else, about her outings with Harley. It was obvious that Joel, having found out, was feeling slighted.

'Oh, someone saw you together, and when I phoned your flat once your mother said you were out. When I hazarded a guess as to who with, she confirmed it.'

'I'm sorry, Joel,' Kym said, 'I should have mentioned it.'

'No reason why you should,' he said rather stiffly. 'Does he know about me?'

Kym admitted that he did. 'Yes . . . you see that night you didn't turn up at the Ship and Gun because your car broke down, remember?—well Harley happened to come in, and I had dinner with him.'

'I see,' Joel mused thoughtfully. 'And that's when it all began. There's been something different about you since then. Are you in love with him?'

Kym did not want to lie, but neither could she tell the truth. 'Your earlier conclusion about me was the right one,' she said.

He regarded her steadily. 'When I saw you with Garfield, I was jealous. I knew I wanted to marry you.'

'Is jealousy a basis for marriage?' Kym queried gently. 'It doesn't prove you're in love with me.'

'It isn't just that, Kym. I've been feeling on edge about our relationship for some time. I knew I was getting too fond of you but I didn't want to stop seeing you.' He laughed. 'Maybe I'm not the bachelor type after all. Maybe we all try not to get hooked too soon because we know we will sooner or later!'

Kym considered him dispassionately. Was it likely that a man who was jealous of Harley, and who disliked him for other reasons, would want to take his child under his own roof? Kym was not sure Joel had sufficient depth of character for that.

'I have to think carefully before I marry,' Kym said, 'It isn't just myself I have to think of. It's Simon too.'

'Simon . . . oh, yes, Simon.' Joel seemed quite relieved. 'He's no problem.'

'He's another man's son,' Kym pointed out, searching his face for clues to his real feelings.

Joel shrugged. 'I like kids,' he said. 'We'd have some of our own, too, I hope.'

Kym suddenly felt irritated with him. He was being too offhand about it. She would rather he had admitted that the situation might have its difficulties. It showed he had not thought about it, not seriously. It occurred to her suddenly that, despite having said he liked children, he had made little effort to get to know Simon. He had never offered to take them both out somewhere. He was willing enough to take Simon on, perhaps, but there had been no warmth in his remarks. And when he had children of his own, would Simon have to take a back seat? Joel wouldn't even know he was hurting the boy, or her. That was the trouble, she realised all at once, Joel was just a bit insensitive.

'You're rushing ahead a bit,' Kym said quietly.

He pulled a face. 'Am I? I suppose I have been thinking ahead a bit lately, seeing it all—you and me—together.' He smiled winningly. 'Marriage never appealed to me before I met you.'

'Joel,' Kym said, choosing her words carefully because she was anxious not to hurt him, 'I'm very fond of you, but I don't think I could marry you. This has nothing to do with you, only with me. Please understand.'

'Have you ever thought that the best way to forget might be to get married again?' he asked persuasively. 'With another man in your bed you'd have to put him out of your mind.'

She shook her head. 'No, it doesn't work like that, Joel. To marry hoping you'll fall in love with your husband is the silliest mistake anyone can make. It could only bring unhappiness to both.'

'Maybe I should have waited a little longer,' Joel said regretfully.

'Can't we just carry on as we are,' suggested Kym, trying to soften her refusal a little. 'Let's see what happens. I don't think either of us ought to rush into anything until we're quite sure.'

There was a tightening of his expression, and then with biting sarcasm that was as unexpected as it was sharp, he said, 'You mean you want to wait and see whether Harley Garfield will ask you to marry him. He's a much better catch than I am. I suppose I can hardly blame you for being ambitious.'

Kym was deeply shocked by this outburst. Joel was always so unaggressive. It seemed to prove that he really was jealous, but that didn't mean he loved her, as she had already told him. She bit back the quick retort that flew to her lips, and instead, keeping her voice level, she answered, 'That was a very unfair thing to say, Joel, and it isn't true. Besides, you should know as well as anyone else, that if Harley Garfield marries anyone, it's most likely to be Lucinda Raymond. He's the ambitious one.'

Joel pursed his lips, and then impetuously clasped her hands. 'I'm sorry, Kym. That was a rotten thing to say. I don't know what came over me.' He laughed self-consciously. 'But I told you, I'm jealous of the man. I don't like you going out with him. I know I can't stop you going out with whoever you like, I have no special claims on you, but I know his reputation, and I just don't like the thought of him kissing you, mauling you . . .'

'You're too imaginative,' Kym told him, 'Like the rest of St A's!'

'Maybe.' He looked at her steadily, then abruptly stood up. 'Another drink?' She nodded and he scooped their glasses together with a flourish.

Kym was not altogether surprised that after that evening she saw less of Joel. Nothing was said, but it was obvious that he was drifting away. She heard on the grapevine that he was taking one or two other nurses out, and although she missed him because, in a way, he provided a buffer between her and her feelings for Harley, and she did like him quite a lot, she was not altogether sorry. She sighed over the whole silly business sometimes. What a paradox it was! Harley had wanted her to marry him because he wanted Simon, not her. Joel had asked her to marry him because he was jealous of Harley, but he only wanted her, she knew, not Simon. And she was sure he would want Simon even less if he knew the boy was Harley's son. For that reason alone she could never marry Joel.

'If only there was someone who wanted us both, just for ourselves,' she thought wistfully, 'and I could fall in love with him!'

About this time she began to worry about her mother. At first there was nothing startling to disturb her, except that a rather bad cold seemed to take a long time to clear up. As time went on Kym noticed a frequent listlessness in Irene which was uncharacteristic of the usually energetic woman. She missed a few of the daytime meetings she had taken to attending, and occasionally dropped out of her evening classes in pottery.

Eventually Kym asked her if she was feeling well. She got the usual retort. 'Oh, that's the trouble with having a nurse in the family. You're always looking for symptoms!'

'It's our job,' said Kym, 'and you've not been yourself lately. I think you should have a check-up.'

'It's just the warm weather,' Irene insisted. 'It's been a bit humid. There's no need to be alarmist.'

'I'm not being. You haven't had a check-up for ages.'

Irene was impatient with her. 'I don't need one! I'm quite sure I haven't got blood pressure or anything like that. I feel fine, Kym.'

Kym let it rest for the time being. She knew better than to try and coerce her mother. A few days later, however, she noticed a bottle of general tonic in the cupboard, but it was not a prescription. Her mother had not been to a doctor. A week or so later she noticed how thin her mother was getting, and she began to worry in earnest. She mentioned it to Harley.

'She is definitely debilitated,' she said anxiously, 'but she won't admit it. And a few days ago I noticed she's got a nasty boil on her neck. She refuses to do anything about it, says it will go, that she's had them before. I think she's very run down.'

He frowned. 'Anything else?'

'Well, she did have a rather lingering bad cold some

time back. It took ages to clear up and she kept having minor relapses, a bit like flu.'

'Mmmm. Any cuts or abrasions slow to heal?'

Kym showed surprise. Then she said thoughtfully, 'Yes . . . as a matter of fact she had a graze on her leg. She snagged it on a supermarket trolley, and she's had a bandage on it for quite a while. She wouldn't let me dress it, she said it was nothing. She's very independent. I might as well not be a nurse for all she'll let me help.'

He nodded. 'Families either exploit or resent having a medical person around. I don't suppose you've any idea if she passes more urine than usual?'

Kym was not sure where this was leading. 'No . . . Though wait a minute, I have heard her get up in the night, and she was saying one day that the trouble with old age is that you need to go to the toilet more often! Of course she's not old . . . she's only just sixty.'

'I think she ought to have some tests,' Harley advised.

'You're thinking it might be diabetes, aren't you?' Kym said, reflecting on his questions.

'It could be any number of things,' he replied noncommittally. 'Can you get her to come down to the hospital?'

'I've tried to get her to go to our local doctor—he's very nice, I've taken Simon there a couple of times—but she won't go. She insists there's nothing wrong with her.'

'I'll talk to her,' Harley offered. 'She might be less nervous about consulting me.'

Kym was grateful. 'Would you?' Then she added hastily, 'I don't like to ask you to do that . . .'

'I'm not aware that you did,' he said, smiling, 'and anyway, I'm practically part of the family, aren't I?'

Kym said nothing, and he patted her hand reassuringly. 'Leave it to me.'

She might have known Harley would succeed where she had failed. He persuaded Irene to go along to the hospital where he personally would check her over. Kym smiled to herself. He could get anyone to do just about anything for him, that man.

'I didn't like to refuse,' Irene told her later. 'He said they're doing some sort of research survey and they need people from all different age groups. And I suppose as I haven't had a check-up for a while and you're always fussing about it, I might as well.'

Kym laughed. 'Go on . . . you fancy him, that's the real reason you're going!'

'I wish *you* did!' Irene retorted. She added diffidently, 'You don't seem to be seeing Joel so much lately. Does that mean you prefer Harley?'

'No, it means Joel prefers certain other young and very pretty nurses,' Kym said without rancour.

'Oh, I see.' Her mother was obviously disappointed.

'I'm not upset,' Kym assured her. 'We were just good friends, as they say. And there are plenty of other unattached young medicos around if I feel lonely!' she added flippantly.

The day her mother went down to St Alphage's for her check-up, Kym waited anxiously for the verdict. Harley had said he would send for her as soon as he had seen her mother. For once they were not too busy on Katherine, the women's medical ward Kym had been on for a week or two. Several patients had been discharged that day and as yet no new ones admitted, so time dragged.

Eventually, however, Sister beckoned to Kym and told her that Dr Garfield wanted to see her in his office. Naturally she seemed a little curious about the summons but Kym did not enlighten her. The less people knew about her association with Harley the better, she felt. She had been seen out with him once and that had caused a ripple of interest for a day or two, but she had remained very noncommittal and the interest waned. There was always something else to gossip about in a big hospital.

Only Gemma occasionally tried a probe, probably

because she knew they had gone around together years ago. She was sure that romance had been revived, despite Kym's protestations. 'I think you're a bit of a dark horse, Kym,' she accused once, then laughed as she added, 'Don't forget to invite me to the wedding, will you? Remember, I'm the one who gave you the idea of coming back here.'

And I wish you hadn't, Kym often thought.

Now as she went up in the lift, her thoughts were not, for once, concerned with Harley, but with her mother. When she entered his office she was surprised to find that her mother was not also there.

'Sit down, Kym,' Harley said, rising briefly as she entered, then sitting down again himself, behind the desk. He leaned his elbows on the desk and laced his fingers together, facing her with a steady, rather serious gaze.

'What's wrong with Mum?' Kym asked, searching his face for the answer before he spoke, certain now that it was not just a case of her mother being a bit run down.

'It is diabetes, I'm afraid,' he told her. 'But we shall know for certain when we've got the results of all our tests.'

'Oh . . .' She had been afraid of this verdict after what he had said previously. But the full implications did not strike her even now. Her mother had never been ill for as long as she could remember, and the fact of her having a serious complaint was difficult to absorb. 'How serious?' she asked fearfully.

'I'm afraid there may be renal complications,' he said gravely.

'But she will recover, won't she?' Kym asked bleakly.

He smiled. 'She's not seriously ill, Kym, so don't worry. If treatment had been delayed much longer, however, it might have been a different story. But of course she won't recover, exactly. She will lead a normal, or near normal life again, but she will be dependent on insulin.'

'Yes . . . yes, of course,' Kym said. Her mind seemed to have gone temporarily blank.

'There's no cause for alarm,' Harley repeated gently. 'So don't let her see how anxious you are, if you can help it.'

'No . . . of course I won't.' Kym felt relief wash over her. It was all right. Diabetes might not be curable, but it was controllable. There was no need to worry. Her mother would be all right.

Harley said slowly, 'I'm afraid we might have to keep her in hospital for some time, Kym.'

At once a new panic seized Kym. She depended utterly on her mother to look after Simon while she worked. Who was going to take him to school and collect him now? Who would get his meals? And who would be there when she was on occasional night shifts, as she had been lately, to help out. All at once it seemed an impossible situation had mushroomed.

'How long will she be hospitalised?' she asked apprehensively.

'Several weeks, I should think, while we deal with the symptoms and side effects and adjust the insulin dosage she'll need.' He smiled at her sympathetically. 'You're on Katherine ward at present, aren't you? That's fortunate. I don't think there's any rule against a nurse tending her own mother, and it would be very reassuring for Irene to have you around. I've arranged for her to be admitted right away.'

'You mean she can't even go home first?' Kym's anxiety renewed itself.

'She could, but I see no point. She might as well save herself the effort. You can bring in whatever she needs.' He went on, 'She's very anxious of course about you and making sure Simon is collected from school . . .'

'Oh, I'll manage somehow,' Kym said. She glanced at

her watch. 'I'll have to pick Simon up myself.' She
pursed her lips worriedly. 'I'd better see Sister right
away about going early, and I'd like to see Mum . . .'
Her voice was taking on a panicky note again.

Harley stood up and came round to her side of the
desk. 'Now, don't get all het up, everything's been
attended to. I've phoned Mrs White and she's collecting
Simon and taking him back to my place.' He paused,
holding Kym's eyes in a steady gaze for a moment or
two. He was not going to stand for any argument, the
expression said. He went on crisply, 'I've told your
mother that she has nothing to worry about regarding
Simon or you, and who will look after you, because I
will.'

Kym's mouth dropped open. 'You!'

A rather self-satisfied little smile was playing about his
mouth. 'Yes . . . or to be more specific, Mrs White will.
You are to move into my house right away.'

Kym felt as though she was going to explode. 'I can't
do that!'

His eyes narrowed slightly. 'What else can you do?
Can *you* afford a housekeeper or an *au pair*? And think
of the trouble getting someone you know you can trust as
implicitly as you do your mother. Mrs White is quite
happy to move in for a while, and you know she's
reliable. So, unless you'd rather stay alone in the flat,
you might as well move in too and be with your son.' He
added, with a bland smile, 'You'll be very adequately
chaperoned!'

Kym felt knocked sideways, and she was infuriated by
his high-handed behaviour. 'You can't just march in and
re-arrange my life!' she objected strongly. 'You can't
just ride roughshod over me like this, organising everything without so much as asking me . . .' Words failed
her.

He replied mildly, 'I'm only trying to help.'

Kym pursed her lips and regarded him suspiciously.

'Why are you doing it, Harley?' she demanded.

He held out his hands helplessly. 'I confess I expected a little more gratitude than this for solving your problems before you even knew they existed!'

'You might at least have consulted me first,' she said sullenly.

'I had the feeling that a *fait accompli* would waste less time,' he said rather dryly. 'You are such an argumentative young lady, and I'm afraid you don't always know what's best for you.'

'You do, of course,' she retorted.

'In this instance, I believe I do,' he rejoined, and after a long speculative look at her, added, 'You can be sure I won't try to coerce you into anything you don't want.'

'Huh,' she scoffed. 'It looks as though you already have.'

'I meant that I won't try to seduce you!' he said, laughingly, but with a touch of asperity.

Kym muttered fiercely, 'And your promises are worth a lot!'

He chuckled softly. 'Kym . . . you are determined not to see my better side, aren't you? Try and credit me with at least a little common humanity—on this occasion. I'm only trying to do you a good turn.'

Kym eyed him narrowly. 'And do yourself one, too? You like the idea of having Simon under your roof, don't you?'

He looked only momentarily disconcerted. 'All right, I admit I am delighted at the opportunity to have my son in my house where I can see him more often for a while. It's an unexpected but welcome bonus.'

Kym heaved a sigh. He wouldn't be so generous, she felt sure, if it weren't for Simon. He had seen his opportunity and seized it. A sudden shiver of fear ran through her. Was he ruthless enough to try and take Simon away from her? She glanced at him, and met his cool steely gaze. Harley Garfield was used to getting his own way. She stamped on her fears resolutely. There was no need for them. He could not take Simon away from her, and he knew it.

He said, 'I'll drive you home after you finish your shift, and after dinner I'll take you over to the flat and you can sort out what your mother will need in hospital, and your own and Simon's things.'

'You don't waste time, do you?' Kym said, through gritted teeth. 'You've worked it all out.' He had purposely, she felt sure, allowed her no time to think it over, refuse his offer, or make arrangements for herself. But could she have done so anyway? It would have been well nigh impossible to find a suitable nannie for Simon in a hurry, even if she could afford it. The alternative would be to stop work and look after Simon herself. She considered that possibility briefly. If she stood her ground right now and refused Harley's offer, she would only be making things awkward for herself, and she knew her mother would think her very ungrateful and pig-headed. Kym did not want to add to her mother's worries unnecessarily. It looked as though she had no alternative but to comply with Harley's arrangements.

'Where is Mum now?' Kym asked. 'Can I see her?'

'Of course, my dear. She's still in the examination room. You can take her back down to Katherine and see her comfortably settled yourself. I'll warn Sister of the situation. Does she know your mother was here for a check-up?'

Kym shook her head. 'No . . . I didn't mention it, and she didn't ask why you wanted to see me.'

'I'll tell her I'm a friend of the family,' he said, 'but perhaps it might be as well not to broadcast your new domestic arrangements.' His eyes were twinkling, and there was a look of satisfaction in them that Kym found a little disconcerting.

'I'll tell Mum to be discreet,' she said, and with

a sidelong look, 'you don't want your reputation be-smirched any more than it is, do you?'

He laid a hand on her arm. 'You do like to get at me, don't you?'

Kym moved out of range. 'Just remember what you promised, that's all.'

'Like the sign on the fruit barrow,' he said, laughing, 'don't squeeze me till I'm yours!' Kym saw fit not to reply to that remark, and turned to go.

She found her mother having a cup of tea, and quite perky, although she looked pale and a little apprehen-sive. To Kym's surprise she did not protest when she told her she was to be admitted right away. In fact she seemed quite relieved, and all she said as they went down to the women's ward together, was:

'I'm glad I came, Kym.'

It was a curious experience for Kym, admitting her own mother to Katherine ward, and she felt quite emo-tional about it. Saying all the reassuring things she had learned, carrying out all the routine functions, seemed very strange when it was your own mother you were dealing with. Irene, for her part, seemed quite bemused by the situation.

'I feel so relieved that everything is all right,' she said happily. 'It was a constant worry to me what you would do if I were really ill. But Harley has really turned up trumps, hasn't he?' She added with conviction, 'He must be fond of you. He wouldn't put himself out like this otherwise.'

'Don't read anything too personal into it, Mum,' Kym warned, and added as offhandedly as she could, 'You won't mention the arrangement in the ward, will you? Harley won't want it spread around the hospital that he's got one of the staff nurses living in his house. Gossip spreads like wildfire in a place like this, and people love jumping to the wrong conclusions.'

'No, dear, I won't breathe a word,' her mother promised. 'I quite understand that it might be embarrassing for you, working here.' She sank back on her pillows. 'I've always wondered what you did all day and now I'll find out!'

Kym chuckled. 'I suppose you'll take delight in reporting me to Sister if I don't jump to it when you want something!'

Irene smiled affectionately, reached for Kym's hand and squeezed it. 'Darling, I know you're a good nurse and Harley says so too. One of the best, he told me. He said you would have been a sister by now if you hadn't been away from it for so long.'

Kym flushed. 'That was kind of him to say so.'

'He is kind,' said Irene with emphasis. 'He'd make a lovely husband, Kym.'

Kym was firm. 'Listen, Mum, you must believe me, there's no chance that Harley and I will ever be more than just friends. Can we let it rest at that?'

Her mother nodded but said hopefully, 'Maybe living in the same house for a while will give you both other ideas.'

CHAPTER EIGHT

IT WAS with very mixed feelings that Kym stepped into Harley's car when she had finished her shift that day. He greeted her cheerfully and enquired how her mother had settled in.

'Is she very upset about having to stay in hospital?'

'Surprisingly, no,' Kym told him. 'I think she's glad it finally came to a head. She was so afraid that if she was really ill it would complicate things for me. She just wouldn't admit that sooner or later she might have to give in. She tried to believe she was just a bit run down and that she would get better if she took a tonic.'

He nodded. 'A common belief of mothers is that they can't afford to be ill.'

Kym said, 'I feel I've burdened her too much.' She sighed deeply. 'I owe her a great deal I can never repay.' She paused, and glanced at him. 'You, too, I admit I hate being under an obligation but there doesn't seem to be any other solution . . .'

He laughed, mockingly, 'You could always change your mind and marry me!' He dropped a hand briefly onto her knee, but he said no more. He took his hand away and started the engine.

Kym was startled. It was the first time he had mentioned the subject in weeks. She had been convinced he had given up the idea. In fact she suspected that his remark now had only been to aggravate her. He must know she was not likely, suddenly, to capitulate.

'Why?' she said. 'Because I owe it to my mother? That sounds like a rather despicable kind of blackmail.'

He manoeuvred the car into the traffic. 'I realise it

would take more than blackmail to change your mind once it's made up!'

'You don't really want me to change my mind,' she said. 'You just like taunting me.'

'You know so much about me it's a wonder you don't write a book about it!' he said, recklessly veering into an inside traffic lane, and braking sharply at the traffic lights.

Kym was briefly thrown against him and felt the power of contact with him involuntarily. 'There's no need to lose your temper with the traffic,' she said tersely.

'You are enough to make a saint lose his temper,' he said through clenched teeth. As the lights were changing, he glanced at her. 'I'm not going to ask you again. This is the last time!'

'I'm glad to hear it,' Kym replied in a brittle tone. 'I'm a bit sick of repeating myself!' She was surprised to find that she had been wrong and marriage was still on his mind, but at least now she knew where she stood. He had just made that quite clear.

He muttered something under his breath which she did not catch, and an uneasy silence descended on the car. After a moment he snapped on the cassette player and filled the car with loud, defensive music. If this was a sample of things to come, Kym thought dismally, pity help them all. There was going to be no harmony at Lowther Square whilst she and Simon were living there. She sat tense and apprehensive as Harley flagrantly disregarded traffic rules and vented his annoyance on his fellow motorists. At every set of traffic lights, she was jolted forwards, straining on her seat belt as they stopped abruptly, and jolted again as he took off precipitately, seconds before the lights changed.

'You'll get run in if you aren't careful,' she ventured once.

'Are you trying to tell me how to drive?' he snapped.

Kym was silent. He was in a thoroughly bad mood,

and she had the horrible feeling it might be because he was regretting having invited her into his home.

At the flat Kym collected a few of Simon's things and her own, flinging them hurriedly into a suitcase and a couple of holdalls. She also gathered together a few items she knew her mother would want. Harley sat morosely in the lounge reading a magazine while she was occupied.

'I'm ready,' she said briskly, rejoining him, and dumping the bags in the hall. 'Shall we go?'

'You've got everything you need?' He seemed less scratchy now as he looked doubtfully at her bags. 'That's not much.'

'Enough for the time being, thanks. I can come back and fetch anything I've forgotten.' Kym added pointedly, 'We're not exactly moving house.'

'No,' he said blandly, 'of course not.'

He stood up, looking down at her, an unfathomable expression on his face, and Kym's heart raced as it always did when he looked at her like that, with something like real tenderness in those passionate blue-grey eyes.

She did not move when he reached out and cupped her face in his large warm hands. Instantly, trickles of fire were scorching through her veins, as his smooth confident kiss caught her off guard, and she became responsive in spite of herself. One hand slid to her waist and pulled her hard against him, awakening a faint desire in them both. Then he let her go, giving her ear a light tug, and kissing the end of her nose.

'I wish you weren't quite so irresistible,' he complained, simmering sensuousness still lingering in his eyes.

Kym turned abruptly away from him, angry that she had let him throw her feelings into turmoil yet again. 'And I wish,' she stated angrily, 'that you wouldn't keep doing that! I've agreed to come and live in your house while my mother is ill, but it's got to be on one condition, that you don't molest me!'

'That's a difficult condition to agree to,' he said mildly, and laughing gently at her. 'You know how I am about promises . . .'

Kym was adamant. 'Well, this time either you keep your promise, or I won't come!' Her eyes flashed at him. She was determined.

He came up and placed his hands on her shoulders. 'All right, I'll try.'

'That's not good enough.'

His lips thinned into an expression of amused reluctance. 'I promise, cross my heart.' He added a trifle resentfully, 'You're a very warm-blooded, sensuous woman, Kym, and you're wasting yourself . . .'

She glanced at him disdainfully. 'I have no intention of wasting myself on you!'

'On Joel Masters perhaps?' he said, an edge to his voice.

'Why don't you mind your own business,' Kym retorted. 'Shall we go? Simon and your housekeeper will wonder what's keeping us.' She bent to pick up the suitcase and his hand closed over hers and took it from her. Even that brief contact set her nerves tingling and she wondered again if she would be able to stand living with him in the same house. It wasn't that she really had any choice, she reflected ruefully. He had organised it all, and what in fact was her alternative?

'I'll take that,' he said, and picked up the larger of the two holdalls as well, leaving Kym to bring the other one and to switch out the lights and lock the door behind them.

'I mustn't forget to come back and defrost the fridge,' she said, more to herself than to him as they went downstairs. 'I've brought all the perishables so it will keep until my next day off, I suppose.'

'Let me know when that is and I'll run you over,'

Harley offered. He seemed to have reverted to good humour.

Kym made a firm refusal. 'No, Harley. You're already doing more than anyone could be expected to, and I'm not going to impose on you for every little thing. I can quite easily come here by tube and I'll get a taxi back to Lowther Square if I need to.'

'Your independence is one of the things I like about you,' he said, with a laugh. 'Even if it is infuriating!'

'I don't intend to be indebted to you more than I absolutely need to be,' she declared.

When the car swung into Lowther Square a few minutes later, and stopped outside the house, Kym glanced up at the lighted windows and wished she felt less uncomfortable about staying there. There was no way, she felt certain, that she was going to enjoy this interlude, no way she would ever feel at ease in Harley's house. All it would do would be to underline the difference between her normal way of life and Harley's. They were, she acknowledged, worlds apart. Although he desired her as a woman, he must realise that too.

She almost felt sorry for him again. The discovery that he had a son had been a great shock, and it must have cost him dearly to offer to marry her. Even though the gesture had been an impetuous one, he must have been well aware of the sacrifice he was making. She had to admire him for that. Some men would not even have contemplated overturning their lives for the sake of an illegitimate son. There was so much that was admirable about Harley. If only underneath it all there was a loving heart—for her.

Kym dismissed that thought instantly. There was no future in wishing for the moon. While she stayed in Harley's house she would have to try harder than ever to regard him dispassionately.

Simon ran to greet her when they entered. He was almost beside himself with excitement. This was the first time he had been to Lowther Square, and it was obvious at once that coming here to live was the most thrilling thing that had ever happened to him. It surpassed even the plane trip from Australia.

'Uncle Harley's got a cat, and there's a goldfish pond in the garden,' he informed Kym breathlessly, eyes shining. 'And Mrs White says . . .' Here he looked hopefully at Harley '. . . she said if I asked you nicely you might fix up a swing on the oak tree at the bottom of the garden. There's a branch that's just right.'

Harley laughed and rumpled his hair. 'Why not? I'll see what I can do.'

'You mustn't bother Uncle Harley too much, Simon. He's doing us a very great favour letting us live here while Nan is sick,' Kym said.

Simon looked momentarily chastened, then he said wistfully, 'We've never lived in a house before, with an upstairs and a garden and . . .' He ran out of breath, and finished, '. . . and everything!'

It was true. Although her parents had owned a house, when Kym and her mother had moved to Australia, they had lived in flats for convenience, and for the same reason they had preferred a flat in London. Kym had often regretted the necessity for this and had promised herself that one day she would try to save enough money to buy a house so that Simon could have a garden to play in. She had always taken him to parks to play but that wasn't the same.

'I'll show you where you can make a tree-house tomorrow,' Harley said. 'There are some old boxes in the garage we can use.'

'Great!' said Simon, delighted.

Kym said, 'I hope you aren't going to spoil him too much.'

Harley grinned at her. 'Another condition?'

She did not have the chance to answer because Mrs White came through from the kitchen to greet them. She clasped Kym's hands in hers. 'My dear, it's lovely to meet you at last! I'm so sorry about your poor mother, I hope it isn't too serious.'

Kym glanced at Harley who explained, 'I'm afraid she'll be in hospital for a few weeks and then she'll need to take things easy for a while.'

'Don't you worry,' said Mrs White firmly to Kym. 'We'll take good care of her, and young Simon.'

'It's tremendously good of you,' Kym said, feeling inadequate because she did not know how to thank the woman, or Harley. 'I would have been in a very awkward spot without Harley's kind offer.'

Mrs White glanced over her shoulder. 'You'll have to excuse me for a minute. I must see to the dinner. Harley will show you your room, dear. Simon's is right next door. I hope you'll be happy with the arrangement.'

'I'm sure I will,' Kym said thankfully. 'Thank you very much for everything.'

Mrs White turned back as she was leaving them. 'Oh, Harley, dear, I almost forgot. There's an urgent message for you on the table there. Would you ring that number?'

He turned and picked up the message pad from the telephone table. His face clouded and his brows knitted in a frown of annoyance. 'Damn!' he said with some feeling.

'What is it? Do you have to go out?' Kym asked anxiously.

He looked at her, then laughed. 'No . . . but I'd better make this call right away. I have a feeling something a bit unexpected has come up. You can remember where the guest room you slept in before was, I expect? Top of the stairs and turn right.'

'I'll show you,' offered Simon, dragging at Kym's hand. 'I know where it is.'

Kym was happy to find herself in the same room where she had slept previously, that fateful first night Harley had taken her out. It was a pretty room with its varying shades of lilac, prettier than any bedroom she had ever had, she thought, looking around it admiringly, and more luxurious too. Her feet seemed to sink into the deep pile carpet.

Simon's room was as big as hers and he was delighted with it, bouncing up and down on the bed in his enthusiasm. Kym was obliged to give him a lecture on how to treat other people's property.

'Uncle Harley won't let us stay here if you don't behave yourself,' she remonstrated. 'So just be careful and don't break anything, or make a mess.'

He flung himself full length on the bed in a rigid pose. 'Yes, Mum,' he said patiently. 'I won't even blink my eyes!'

Kym couldn't help a smile. Even at six years old he had a flair for sly mockery, like his father. She looked down at him as he grinned at her, peeping at her from under lowered lashes, and he looked so like Harley she winced, and turned away.

'You'd better wash your hands, young man,' she said, 'it's time for dinner.'

Over dinner there was a general round-the-table discussion about the new household routines. Kym was firmly reassured that she had nothing to worry about concerning Simon. Mrs White was happy to take him to, and collect him from school each day, even though it meant a fairly long journey for her. She had her own car, she said, and it would be no trouble at all.

'Dr Garfield is very generous to me,' she confided privately to Kym later, and at that Kym felt a pang of guilt. Harley was no doubt paying Mrs White quite a bit more to look after Simon. It made her feel more indebted to him than ever, but she knew that if she offered to meet the cost herself, her offer would be dismissed out of hand.

However, conscience forced her to mention it when they were on their way back to the hospital to visit her mother, but as she expected he merely said in a crisply dismissive tone, 'You don't object to my doing something for my son, do you?'

'No . . . of course not,' she conceded meekly.

Irene was looking perkier than she had for some time, Kym thought when she walked into the ward. A decision had been taken for her, and she was now relaxed. Her proper medication would not begin until tomorrow when the results of all today's tests would be known, Harley had told Kym. He did not accompany her to see her mother because, as he said, 'The gossips have quite enough to gnaw on. The less we are seen together the less speculation there will be.'

Kym agreed and was glad, in any case, to see her mother alone.

Irene's face lit up at the sight of her. 'Kym . . . I didn't expect you to come back tonight.'

'I brought a few things I thought you might need,' Kym told her. 'Your reading glasses and that novel you were half way through.' She put them on the bedside table and stowed the remainder of the items in the cupboard underneath. 'I've brought you a couple of clean nighties and a bed jacket too. You'll feel better in your own rather than that hospital gown. Do you want to change now? I can pull the screens around.'

Irene shook her head. 'No . . . I'm quite comfortable as I am. No need to disturb everything now.' She leaned forward. 'And how do you like being at Harley's place? Is it very grand?' she asked in a low voice.

'It is a bit,' admitted Kym with a smile. 'Not our style at all. But Simon, of course, adores it. There's a Siamese cat and a garden with a fishpond, and he's got a room of his own that's three times as big as his bedroom at the flat. It'll be hard for him to go back there, I'm afraid.'

Irene said meaningfully, 'Perhaps he won't have to.'

Kym shot her a warning look. 'Now, Mum . . .'

Irene just smiled and Kym knew it was no use arguing

with her since she was convinced that Harley was keen on her daughter. However, she felt obliged to say, 'Mum, I do wish you would realise that Harley's being kind, that's all. He's provided a temporary solution to a problem and I'm immensely grateful for it, but it's no more than that.' Momentarily she toyed with the idea of telling her mother right now what the real situation was but in the middle of the ward, with other patients liable to overhear her, it was hardly the time or place.

She stayed and chatted for a few minutes, but as it was after visiting hours and the night staff were anxious to settle the ward down for the night, she did not linger. Her mother seemed a bit sleepy now anyway, so Kym kissed her and slipped away, pausing only for a few minutes to talk to the night nurse in charge, and to check on her mother's report so far.

Then she made her way down to the car park. Harley was already waiting in the car. By the time they arrived back at Lowther Square it was late and Mrs White had put Simon to bed, and had retired herself. Kym stood uncertainly in the hall, unused to this new situation, and feeling extremely awkward.

'I can only thank you again, Harley,' she said, wishing she did not have to feel so obligated to him.

'You don't have to keep repeating yourself,' he said, leaning against the hall table and regarding her lengthily.

'Well, I'll say goodnight, then,' Kym said, starting towards the stairs.

He took a step, bringing him alongside her. 'Wouldn't you like some coffee?' His eyes dared her.

'No, I really don't think . . .' Kym faltered.

He gave her a half smile. 'You don't mean to completely ostracise me in my own house, I hope. Surely we can co-exist on friendly terms and socialise occasionally even when there isn't a chaperon to protect your virtue.' The slight mockery was there, dancing in his eyes.

'I thought you were probably too tired,' she said evasively.

'I am tired, and so are you, and that's all the more reason to unwind a little with a nightcap. You'll sleep much better, I assure you.'

He caught her arm lightly, and to prevent further protest on her part, guided her into the drawing room. 'Sit down and put your feet up. I'll make the coffee. Won't be a minute. Will instant do?'

'Yes—fine.'

It had been an exhausting day both physically and mentally and she slumped thankfully into a comfortable armchair and lifted her feet wearily onto a nearby stool. She leaned back and looked around the room. How she would love to have a house like this! There wasn't much chance of ever being able to afford this sort of luxury, she thought ruefully, and hoped Simon would not resent her for being unable to provide it. Or the yacht he craved! But it would be wrong to marry Harley, she told herself yet again. She shifted restlessly. Was that question always going to haunt her—would she never be absolutely sure she had done the right thing in refusing him?

She leaned back and closed her eyes, and had almost drifted off when a soft plop on her lap startled her into wakefulness.

'Oh, Kai! You gave me a fright,' she laughed, gazing into the inscrutable blue eyes that observed her penetratingly, as his paws kneaded her stomach prior to curling up on her.

When Harley came back the cat was already curled up and Kym was idly fondling its neck. Harley placed the tray on the table near her, and glanced at Kai. 'Make him get down if he's bothering you.'

'I like cats,' she said, adding with a laugh. 'You must always be careful not to offend them. Otherwise they put a spell on you!'

Harley looked down at her with a gleam in his eyes. 'Mmm . . . I'll have to have a word in his ear about the kind of spell I'd like him to put on you!'

Kym shot him a deliberately arch look. 'And how do you know I haven't got in first with a counter spell?'

He grinned at her. 'Ah, so that's what you're up to. Well, let me tell you, Kai is hopeless at spells! It hasn't worked!'

'Give it time!' Kym said, laughing too.

'Have some coffee,' he said, 'there are biscuits in the tin. Mrs White makes a batch of my favourites every week.' He crossed to the cocktail cabinet and poured two measures of brandy.

Kym said, 'She obviously spoils you.'

'It's very strange,' he mused, 'but people do!'

'Only women, I'll bet!'

He chuckled. 'There is nothing a man likes more than to be spoilt by a woman.' He shot her a sly look. 'And some lucky fellow may be spoilt by you one day, I suppose.'

'Perhaps,' she conceded lightly, taking the glass of brandy he offered her. She went on quickly, 'Now, tell me about my mother.'

He sat on the couch, leaning forward, his brandy glass clasped in his hands held between his knees, warming it. 'I believe she is a fairly normal case of diabetes mellitus . . .'

Kym listened carefully as he described the various characteristics of the disease, and the course that her mother's medication was to take. Once again he assured her that the prognosis was good and that she had no need to worry unduly.

Then he leaned back, crossing one leg over the other in a relaxed way, one foot resting on the other knee. 'There's definitely no cause for anxiety, Kym. She'll be all right once we've adjusted her insulin requirement. The kidney problem is not serious, fortunately. She'll have to learn to give herself the injections, of course, because you can't be on hand to do it all the time, but she'll soon get used to that. She'll be able to lead a perfectly normal life, provided she follows instructions to the letter, doesn't forget her injections, and follows a sensible diet. All those other side effects will clear up in due course. There's no reason why she shouldn't live to be a very old lady. Her heart is quite sound and there's nothing else wrong with her.'

He paused. 'As a matter of fact, I'm personally familiar with diabetes, and I've studied the disease quite thoroughly. My grandmother suffered from it.' He saw the flicker of anxiety that Kym could not disguise, and shook his head. 'No, it wasn't hereditary, as I'm sure your mother's is not. You don't know of any incidence of the disease in the family?'

'No . . .'

'Then I doubt that Simon is at risk. If so it probably would have evidenced itself by now. Diabetes is also one of the diseases of advancing age, but fortunately it is one we can control quite easily. My grandmother lived to be ninety-eight, and it wasn't diabetes that killed her. She fell and broke her hip and developed pneumonia.'

Kym felt a good deal reassured after talking to Harley about her mother's condition. She knew quite a bit about the disease, naturally, but it was good to have an explanation from someone as expert as Harley, especially as she knew he would tell her the truth and not wrap it up in trite phrases. He would have been just as candid with her mother, too, she was sure, and felt glad that he was her physician.

'I've never nursed a diabetic,' she said. 'Is there anything special I should know?'

Harley considered briefly, then gave her a run down on what would be required of her. 'But Sister Barber will instruct you,' he finished, adding, 'She's extremely competent. One of our best sisters.'

Kym could not stifle the yawn that rose to her lips. 'Excuse me . . .' she apologised. 'I think it's time I went to bed. I'll just rinse the mugs. She picked up the tray, but Harley rose and took it from her. 'You're half asleep. It's been a very stressful day for you. I'll do this.'

Kym was insistent, 'You've got to let me do something!'

He shrugged. So, gently moving Kai from her lap, Kym followed him out to the kitchen. She washed the mugs and he wiped them. He told her that she was to feel perfectly free to use the kitchen and any other part of the house as she wished, and that he had told Mrs White that.

'She'll carry on as before and look after Simon for you,' he said, 'but if at any time you want to cook, or whatever, feel quite free to do so. I'm sure you'll be able to work out something satisfactory between you.'

'Thank you. I'm sure Mrs White would appreciate some extra time off now and then,' Kym said. 'Perhaps I could take over the cooking on my days off.'

He smiled in agreement. 'That would be an excellent idea.' He added, with a teasing look, 'If you're only half as good a cook as your mother is, you'll be all right.'

Kym blushed. 'Wait until you've tried my cooking before you pass judgment. Daughters don't always follow in their mother's footsteps.'

'No,' he agreed, 'I daresay they don't.' He had put the tea-towel away and was looking steadily at her as she wiped her hands and hung the towel back on its hook. She could see very plainly that he was fighting a battle with himself to keep away from her, and the knowledge served to stir her own yearnings alarmingly.

'Well, I'm off to bed,' she said lightly, sidestepping past him, through the door. 'Goodnight, Harley.'

He remained where he was. 'Goodnight, Kym,' he said quietly. 'Sleep well.'

Kym hardly expected to, but she was so exhausted she

was asleep the moment her head hit the pillow and she knew nothing more until her alarm clock shrilled in her ear in the morning. Harley drove her to the hospital as they were both on duty at the same time. That would not always be the case, she knew, but as it was less distance by tube from St Alphage's to Lowther Square than it had been to the flat, living in Harley's house was in fact more convenient.

Harley said he would not be available to drive her home that afternoon, as he had to go out that evening straight from the hospital. He did not say where, and Kym naturally did not enquire. His private life was his own.

However, she did say, 'I don't want you to think you have to keep giving me lifts just because I'm living in your house. I do realise you have a life of your own, and Simon and I don't want to interfere with that in any way.'

He gave her a quizzical look. 'Which is the same thing as telling me you have a life of your own and you don't want me interfering in it?'

'If you like,' she replied. She had not admitted yet that she was not seeing Joel any more. She felt it might be wiser to let Harley assume she still was.

Sister Barber was on duty in Katherine ward during Kym's shift that day, and as it was she who had been there when Harley had summoned Kym to his office to give her the verdict on her mother's condition, she was naturally still somewhat curious.

'So Dr Garfield is a friend of your family,' she remarked, and obviously very keen to hear more about it.

Kym said, 'Well, yes, he is . . . it goes back a long way.' She added sunnily, 'He's very kind, isn't he?'

Sister Barber agreed, and pursued the subject no further, much to Kym's relief. So long as no-one knew that she was living temporarily at Lowther Square, the gossips would have nothing much to chew over. Few people knew of her domestic arrangements, but those

who did and were also aware that her mother was in
hospital, naturally asked sympathetically how she was
managing. Sue, on Wren ward was one of them.

'Hard luck your mother getting sick, Kym,' Sue said
when they met in the canteen at lunch time. 'What are
you going to do about Simon?'

Kym was forced to prevaricate. 'Well, it was a bit of a
problem, but fortunately I know someone who's able to
take him to and from school. She'll look after him until I
get home.'

'Well, that sounds all right. I was going to suggest that
my sister might be able to help. She lives quite near you.
She was a nurse, too, but she's married now with a
couple of kids of her own.'

Kym thanked her. 'It's a kind thought, Sue, but I think
I'll be able to manage. Mum might not be in hospital for
too long.'

Sue said thoughtfully, 'It must feel a bit funny having
your own mother on the ward.'

'It does rather,' admitted Kym. 'I know she's got her
eye on me!'

Sue suddenly noticed the time. 'Hey, I'd better fly.
See you later. I want to tell you about a party you're
going to!'

Kym's weak protest made no impression on her
friend, as she knew it wouldn't. Sue was always organising social outings for her, and would never take no for an
answer. She meant well, and Kym appreciated her
concern. It was just that lately she was seldom in the
mood for parties.

That was Harley's fault. It was his fault too that the
next little while was going to be one of constant
apprehension in case anyone found out where she was
living. Some people, like Gemma for instance, were
very inquisitive, and might ask more probing questions
than Sue. Gemma had a gift for sniffing out all kinds of
gossip. And if she did tumble to the truth, there was no

way she would be able to keep it to herself. Kym resolved to avoid her if she could. Since they worked in different areas, she rarely saw Gemma anyway, so she judged it shouldn't be too difficult.

Kym's mother responded to treatment much more quickly than anyone expected, even Harley, and she was soon allowed to go home. Kym was obliged to invent another neighbourly person who had offered to keep an eye on her while she was at work, for those like Sue who solicitously enquired, but to her relief there seemed to be few people at St A's who were interested in her domestic arrangements. Nobody had the least idea that she went home each night to Harley Garfield's house, and if anyone noticed her occasionally arriving with him in the morning, it didn't seem to have occurred to them to make anything of it.

By the time Irene left hospital she was fully adjusted to the correct insulin dosage for her condition and feeling quite fit. Like Kym, she was slightly overawed by the house in Lowther Square, and Kym thought she would never stop admiring it and all it contained. Right from the start she and Mrs White got on like a house on fire, which pleased Kym and seemed to amuse Harley.

It occurred to Kym one day, watching them chatting animatedly together, that previously her mother might have been lonely. She felt guilty about it, and said so to Harley.

'I never thought of it before,' she said. 'She used to go out quite a bit. She joined a couple of clubs and went to lectures on subjects that interest her, after Simon started school, but she never made any really close friends. It never occurred to me that she might be lonely, but now I realise she must have been. She seems to have found a kindred spirit in Mrs White.'

'Which is good for both of them,' he remarked.

Kym laughed suddenly. 'And do you know what

Simon said the other day? He said it was terrific, like having two grandmothers. I don't know whether Mrs White was pleased about that!'

Harley grinned. 'She'd be delighted. She doesn't have any children, so no grandchildren to look forward to, and she loves Simon.'

The household in Lowther Square ticked over so placidly that Kym had to keep reminding herself that it was not permanent. Her mother was almost fully fit again, and yet for some reason she found herself hesitating to broach the subject of their moving back to the flat. It was partly because she dreaded having to tell Simon that they would have to leave. He was so happy here, and inevitably his relationship with his father had become cemented even more firmly. There would be tantrums, she knew, and every time she thought about it, she wished they had never come at all. But, the point was, they couldn't *stay*.

Eventually something happened to force her hand.

One day she sat next to Gemma in the canteen. Or rather Gemma joined her and several other nurses, and in due course the conversation centred around hospital gossip.

'Have you heard the latest about Harley Garfield?' Gemma asked everyone in general, but her eyes were shrewdly gleaming and directed at Kym. She knew Kym had been seen out with Harley once, but when she had asked her casually a while ago if she was still going out with him, Kym had simply laughed and said, 'Oh, you know Harley!' and refused to be drawn.

Now Kym said, 'No, why?' as though she wasn't particularly interested.

'I just wondered if you'd heard the rumour,' Gemma said, her eyes very sharp.

'What rumour?' Kym came in too quickly, and the other girls looked at her curiously.

Gemma, as usual, took full enjoyment out of imparting a piece of gossip. 'Well, it seems Lucinda Raymond came back from America a few weeks ago, and the general consensus is that wedding bells are in the offing. She and Harley Garfield were seen mooning over champagne in the Casablanca Room, and dancing cheek to cheek at the Royal Flush the other night.'

'Who do you know who can afford to take you there!' exclaimed one of the other nurses enviously.

'I wasn't there,' snorted Gemma. 'I happened to hear a couple of the registrars talking about it. I must say it does look as though it's on again, and the Chairman's daughter really is keen on the handsome young consultant.'

'What do you think, Kym?' Gemma asked. 'You must know him better than any of us. You knew him when you were nursing here before.'

Kym was feeling ridiculously churned up inside. She said hollowly, 'I'm sorry, I really don't know anything about it at all.'

Gemma gave her a sympathetic look, and Kym hoped she wouldn't put it around that Nurse Rutherford was a bit piqued, another victim of Harley Garfield's devastating charm and love-them-and-leave-them tactics.

'Maybe she went off to America to make up her mind,' suggested one of the nurses. 'You know, they do say absence makes the heart grow fonder.'

Gemma shrugged. 'I'd have thought that while the cat's away the mice will play would apply more aptly to him!'

'Doubtless it did!' commented someone cynically.

Gemma went on, 'I suppose if he was going to give up his freedom for anyone, it would be for someone like her. She's a stunner.'

'And her father's chairman of the board,' remarked the girl next to Kym, 'as well as being filthy rich. It would seem to be a perfect match.'

'And the end of many a first-year's dreams!' laughed

Gemma. She glanced at Kym. 'You look a bit stunned, Kym. He didn't have you on a piece of string, too, did he?'

Kym snapped out of her private thoughts. 'Me! Good heavens no!' She met Gemma's sharp enquiring eyes levelly and hoped she was giving nothing away in her own expression. If Gemma had the least idea what had been going on, it would be all over the hospital in a trice, and she would feel utterly humiliated, even if people did feel sorry for her.

She was torn between dismay and anger. Lucinda had been back for weeks, according to Gemma, and Harley had not said a word about it. Somehow he must be managing to keep her from coming to the house, as obviously he would not want her to find out that he was providing a roof for a staff nurse and her son, and her mother.

All at once Kym's emotions were in total confusion again. Fortunately the other nurses had to go, and Kym rose, too, thankful to escape back to the ward. For the rest of the day, no matter how hard she tried not to think about it, her mind kept coming back to the same thing. Lucinda was back from America. But she was sure Harley had said she would not be back until October or thereabouts. She must have returned unexpectedly, and Kym guessed it would have been quite a shock for Harley. He would have expected Kym and her family to be gone long before Lucinda was due to return. He had successfully managed to give no sign, however, that he had suddenly found himself in a very awkward predicament because of them.

Kym began to think back over recent weeks, searching for some clue as to just when Lucinda might have returned, but she could not recall any noticeable change in Harley. Then, all at once, she remembered the very night she had moved into Lowther Square. There had been an urgent telephone message for him, and he had looked quite stricken. Could that message have been from Lucinda? Intuitively, Kym felt it must have been.

She felt terrible about the whole thing, and made up her mind to tackle Harley about it at the very first opportunity.

CHAPTER NINE

THE KNOWLEDGE that Lucinda had returned earlier than expected disturbed Kym greatly. She knew that Harley was now in something of a predicament, and that it was her fault. Not her fault directly, but the fact that she and her family were living at Lowther Square was something she felt sure he would have difficulty explaining to Lucinda. She was not the kind of girl to be easily convinced that all was not as it might appear.

Taking the bull by the horns, Kym broached the subject next morning when Harley was driving to the hospital. They had begun by talking about her mother, and Kym said, 'I blame myself . . .'

'What for?' he asked, surprised.

'For ignoring the signs. I should have noticed she was ill ages ago. It's only luck she didn't go into a coma.'

He slid her a meaningful glance. 'Perhaps you were just too busy with your own affairs.'

Kym flinched, knowing he was alluding to Joel. 'That was no excuse . . .' she said soberly.

There was a brief pause, then Harley said, 'I saw Joel Masters in the Ship and Gun the other day. He had a very pretty little girl with him. One of the second-years, I believe.'

Kym just shrugged, 'Very likely.'

Harley's next remark was harshly spoken. 'He's not the sort of man you ought to lose your head over.'

'Who says I have?' she countered.

'You as good as admitted to me you were in love with him,' he said. When Kym did not answer he went on, 'Masters isn't the sort of stepfather I'd like Simon to have.'

Kym bridled. 'So now you're trying to dictate whom I should marry, or not! I don't think you have the right to do that, Harley, even though Simon is your son.'

He was silent but his annoyance with her showed clearly in his grim profile. Nevertheless, Kym suddenly found herself asking brightly, 'Did Lucinda enjoy her trip to America?'

'I believe so,' Harley answered, betraying no surprise that she knew of Lucinda's return even though he had not told her himself.

'I thought you said she wasn't coming back till October,' Kym said.

He did not deny it. 'Lucinda seldom keeps to her plans. It was always on the cards she would tire of gallivanting around over there and come back.'

Kym plunged right in, since the subject was now raised. 'But if you'd known she was going to turn up earlier than you expected you wouldn't have invited us to move in, would you? She must be a bit put out because we're living in your house.'

She watched his face carefully but it revealed nothing. He glanced at her, half smiling now. 'Must she?'

'Well, I would have thought . . .' He had disconcerted her, and Kym wished she had not brought up the subject, after all.

'Lucinda Raymond is not someone you need to think about,' Harley said with emphasis.

Kym protested, 'But I do! And in any case Mum is quite fit now. It's time we went back to our flat, Harley. I'm sure I can find someone willing to take Simon to and from school until Mum's fit enough to take over again. Sue Grant's sister—Sue's on Wren, you know her— might be able to . . .'

'For heaven's sake, Kym, shut up about it,' he snapped impatiently. 'If you were an inconvenience, I'd make alternative arrangements myself. There's no problem, so stop fussing. You are not leaving until I say your mother is fit enough to take on Simon and everything else.'

'I'm not fussing,' said Kym levelly, resenting his high-handed manner, 'but I know how I'd feel in Lucinda's place. She's bound to find out, Harley, if you haven't told her, and you'll have a devil of a job explaining.'

'You are showing a quite unwarranted interest in Lucinda,' he remarked. 'I might almost be tempted into believing you're jealous.'

'Envious perhaps,' agreed Kym frankly. 'Who wouldn't be? She's got everything.'

'Including me,' he put in, with a short ironic laugh, and a swift mocking glance at her as they swept into the hospital forecourt. 'That's what you think, isn't it?'

'Well, hasn't she?' Kym said.

He did not answer her, but said enigmatically, 'Just leave Lucinda to me.' He added, a trifle acidly, 'I believe we agreed not to interfere in each other's private lives.'

Kym accepted the rebuff. She had, after all, only a few minutes ago rebuffed any interference from him. She did not mention Lucinda again, but in spite of herself she could not help thinking about the girl. Harley was often out in the evenings and she presumed mostly with Lucinda. No doubt she had a palatial apartment some-where. Kym would have given anything to know, however, whether Lucinda did know of the arrangement at Lowther Square, and what she thought about it. But Harley rarely said anything about his comings and goings. He certainly seemed to be keeping Lucinda away from the house, and that was all the enlightenment Kym had.

Although she tried not to let it be, the thought of Lucinda in Harley's arms was a thorn in her side, and in the end she had to admit that she was jealous. There she was, living in Harley's house, mother of his son, and yet she was nothing to him except a desirable woman. And even in that regard she was scarcely unique. There must have been, still were probably, plenty of women whom Harley found desirable, and no doubt plenty of them found him irresistible. So far as she was concerned, however, he had kept his promise. Since she had been in the house, his behaviour had been a model of rectitude. That Lucinda's return might be in part responsible for that, she could not ignore.

One afternoon, a few days after her conversation with Harley, Kym arrived home expecting to find an empty house, because she knew Mrs White and her mother had taken Simon to the dentist and it was unlikely they would have returned yet. She was therefore somewhat startled when she opened the front door to hear someone playing the piano in the drawing room. It could hardly be Harley since he was still at the hospital.

The sound of her closing the front door brought the music to a halt, and a moment later Lucinda Raymond appeared in the drawing-room doorway, tall, slender and very chic in a strawberry coloured suede suit, her blonde hair swept up glamorously with not a strand out of place, her make-up flawless. A drift of expensive perfume wafted across the hallway to Kym. She looked younger that she had at their previous encounter.

'Oh, hello . . . you must be Kym,' Lucinda said, a brief flicker of recognition in her eyes. 'Haven't we met somewhere before?' Her voice was high and brittle, and although her lips smiled, her eyes did not at all.

Kym, breathless from hurrying and rather windswept, said, 'Yes . . . in a restaurant in Soho a few months ago. You're Lucinda Raymond, aren't you?'

Lucinda's eyes roved over Kym critically, making a minute examination and sparkling with antagonism. 'Yes, I remember . . . You were with a rather self-conscious young houseman.' She was being bitchy. Joel wasn't self-conscious!

'Joel Masters,' Kym said shortly.

Lucinda shrugged. Names of lesser mortals obviously

meant nothing to her. She did not normally mix with junior medical staff, either doctors or nurses. Her world was outside the hospital anyway. She demanded briskly, 'Where's Harley?'

'I don't know when he'll be home,' Kym said. She could not tell yet whether Lucinda had prior knowledge of the set-up in Lowther Square, or whether she had just accidentally discovered it. Her rather grim expression seemed to suggest the latter. Kym added, 'He did say he might be a bit late this evening.'

Lucinda shrugged. 'Doesn't matter. I'll wait.'

'Is he expecting you?' Kym asked casually.

Lucinda lifted her chin haughtily. 'I didn't actually say I'd drop in but he told me he was planning to stay in this evening. I'm sure he won't mind if I stay to dinner. I'm at a bit of a loose end myself.'

And suspicious, thought Kym, which is why you've come here. She said, 'Will you excuse me for a minute? I feel as though I've been blown inside out. It's very gusty outside.'

Lucinda, who looked as though she had just stepped out of a beauty parlour, gave her a supercilious look that suggested Kym's own description of herself was apt. 'Don't mind me,' she said. 'I wouldn't mind a cup of tea, though.' She added silkily, 'You're going to have one, I suppose?'

'Yes—at least it's no trouble to make one,' Kym said obligingly, and then thought, 'Why doesn't she make it herself? She ought to be familiar enough with things here!' But people like Lucinda Raymond didn't ever make the tea, she decided, if there was someone else to do it.

She sighed and wished Harley was not going to be late. Entertaining Lucinda was not her idea of relaxing after a hard day. She hoped Mrs White and her mother and Simon would not be too long. They would at least be support in numbers.

Kym ran upstairs and tidied herself, then went down to the kitchen and made a pot of tea which she carried into the drawing room, deciding that out of politeness she ought to join the girl. Besides, she had no intention of letting Lucinda think she was any less a guest in Harley's house than she was. It was with a little trepidation, however, that she set the tray on the table and poured the tea. How much did Lucinda know?

She soon found out.

Lucinda took the fine bone-china cup and saucer in slender fingers with scarlet tips, crossed her knees elegantly, and said in a deceptively level voice, 'I had a nice long chat to your mother before they had to go out. I met your son, too.'

'Mum and Mrs White were taking Simon to the dentist's,' Kym said conversationally. 'He's been having a bit of trouble lately with his second teeth coming through before the milk teeth fall out. They're a bit crooked and he might need a brace for a while.' She knew Lucinda was not the slightest bit interested in Simon's teething problems but nervousness was making her rattle on.

Lucinda's lip curled slightly. 'Your mother told me how Harley had offered to let you live here while she was in hospital, and until she's quite fit again.'

Her tone revealed that this had been news to her. Kym noted it and replied quietly, 'It really is very generous of him, isn't it? We do feel so obligated.'

The light blue eyes flickered dangerously. 'Harley told me the decorators were in!' she said scathingly. 'I came round to see how the work was progressing!'

Kym, suppressing a sudden desire to laugh, said loyally, 'I hope you're not getting any wrong ideas about all this, Lucinda. I suppose Harley didn't tell you about it because he didn't want you to think . . .'

Lucinda gave a shrill burst of laughter. 'Of course he didn't! He knows I'm not that easily hoodwinked.'

'Truly, it isn't the sort of set-up I can see you do think it is,' said Kym earnestly. 'Ask Mrs White.'

Lucinda sneered. 'How would she know what the set-up is?'

'Well, you'll have to take my word—and Harley's—for it,' said Kym matter-of-factly.

Lucinda tapped a long slender finger on the edge of her saucer. Her eyes never left Kym's face and she was unable to conceal her dislike.

'Your mother said you'd only recently returned from Australia,' she remarked.

'A few months ago now,' Kym acknowledged, wondering where this was leading.

'You were married out there?' Lucinda's tone was dangerously sweet.

'Yes.'

'How very sad for you to have been widowed so young. It must have been a tragic blow.' There was little sympathy in her tone.

Kym said nothing, but fixed her gaze on the carpet, waiting for Lucinda's next question, which was: 'Did you know Harley before you went to Australia?'

'He was at St Alphage's when I did my nursing training there,' Kym told her.

Lucinda's eyes glittered. 'I see.' She glanced around the room. 'I don't suppose you've been used to this . . . this kind of living.'

'My mother and I live very comfortably, but we don't usually enjoy quite this luxury, I'm afraid,' admitted Kym honestly.

The glint in Lucinda's eyes hardened and there was a sting in her voice. 'It must be very tempting to imagine yourself in these sort of surroundings permanently.'

'Just as soon as my mother is well enough we'll be going back to the flat,' Kym said defensively.

Lucinda placed her cup and saucer carefully back on

the tray. Her blue eyes were piercing. 'Unless you can persuade Harley to marry you!'

'I beg your pardon!' Kym exclaimed indignantly.

Lucinda uncrossed her legs and leaned forward, a certain menace in the beautiful flawless face. 'You're just a little gold-digger, aren't you? And you think you've got the perfect lever to get what you want.'

'What are you talking about?' Kym demanded hotly, infuriated by the tone of her voice as much as by what she had said.

'You know,' said Lucinda. 'I've had time to think about it while I was waiting for you to come home. I knew the minute I set eyes on him that there was something about that child, something vaguely familiar, and then it suddenly dawned on me.' Her lips vanished into a thin hard line and there was open hostility in her eyes. 'Simon is Harley's child, isn't he?'

Kym felt as though she had just received a hard punch in the stomach. She was astounded that Lucinda had guessed so quickly, but with Lucinda's special interest in Harley, perhaps it wasn't too surprising.

'Well,' Lucinda prompted. 'You're not going to try and deny it, are you?'

'No,' said Kym. 'It's true.'

Lucinda folded her arms. 'I thought there was something funny going on. Decorators!' She spat the word out contemptuously. 'I suppose he thought he could sort you out before I got back. Poor Harley! What a shock it must have been for him when you presented him with Simon! The past does have a nasty habit of catching up with one, I suppose.' She eyed Kym curiously. 'I wonder why you didn't tell him in the first place.'

Kym had no intention of explaining her motives to this objectionable girl. She merely said, 'I didn't tell Harley now. He found out.'

'I bet you made it easy for him to do that,' sneered Lucinda. 'What's the difference anyway? You're obviously trying to get him to marry you.'

'As a matter of fact I'm not,' said Kym hotly, and nearly told her that it was Harley who had been trying all along to get her to marry him.

Lucinda clearly would not believe her. 'You're in his house, you've managed to get your foot in the door, and presumably his bed as well. It's my guess you've already threatened to drag his name in the dirt unless he marries you.'

'That's not true!' Kym expostulated.

'I shall see what Harley says about that,' Lucinda said smoothly. 'I think I know him rather better than you do. It was very silly of him not to tell me what was going on. He should have known I would have helped.'

'To do what?' Kym asked, suspiciously.

'To get rid of you, my dear, and your brat and your ailing mother. Don't think you hold all the trump cards. I know how to deal with people like you.' She laughed. 'Money doesn't buy everything, but it buys most things—including people.'

'I'm afraid you're completely off beam,' Kym said, tightlipped. 'I don't want anybody's money.' But she could see that protestations would be useless. Lucinda had formed her own picturesque view of the situation and was not to be deterred from it. She was obviously a strong-willed girl, and Kym wondered idly if Harley would have the strength to resist her, if she wanted something that he didn't. She was very beautiful, very sensuous, and marriage to her would be very advantageous to him. If he had to choose between Lucinda and Simon, and that was what Kym now suspected might prove to be the case, what choice would he make?

She said mildly, 'Would you like some more tea, Lucinda?'

Lucinda indicated impatiently that she would. 'Yes, thanks.' She went on, 'You're a pretty cool customer, I must say. And you do have a certain obvious attractiveness I suppose.' She shrugged and smiled tolerantly. 'And a man is a man. I don't blame Harley for what happened years ago before I even knew him, or even his taking advantage of the fact that I was abroad for several months. We aren't actually engaged yet.' Nevertheless, her expression was smugly magnanimous.

'Harley has not taken advantage of the fact that you were away, at least not so far as I am concerned,' Kym said flatly, and she added pointedly, 'I believe we only moved in about the time you returned, as a matter of fact.' She was gratified to see a slight shift in Lucinda's expression, a shadow of uneasiness.

The girl said airily, 'It doesn't worry me if he had. I'm broadminded. I don't expect a man to be a pillar of virtue. He wouldn't be very interesting if he was. But I can't say I'm keen on the idea of a woman and her illegitimate son making constant demands in the background. Would you be?' she challenged Kym.

'Probably not,' Kym conceded, 'but if . . .'

Lucinda interrupted. 'I've no doubt we can come to some amicable arrangement,' she said, softening a little. 'Would you be willing to fade quietly out of his life if I made it very worth your while? I could probably arrange a nice little Charge Sister's job for you up North, say. My father is pretty influential, you know. And we could agree on some regular . . .'

'Lucinda!' Kym stood up angrily. 'I am sick of this conversation. I think you had better wait until Harley gets home and gives you the true facts, since you are unwilling to believe me.' She glared at her visitor with growing dislike. 'And now, if you'll excuse me, I have things to do!'

She marched across the room, and, at that moment, to her relief, the front door slammed and her mother and Simon came in with Mrs White. Kym met them in the hall. The two women looked at her apprehensively.

Kym was aware that her expression was tense, her face probably pale.

Mrs White whispered, 'Is *she* still here?'

Kym nodded, and they all went out to the kitchen.

Irene said, 'She was very inquisitive. I didn't quite know what I should or shouldn't tell her. It was very difficult . . .'

'Don't worry about it, Mum,' said Kym. 'It doesn't matter.' She turned to Simon. 'How's your tooth, darling?' She tilted her son's pale face and dropped a kiss on her forehead. 'Did it hurt much?'

'Not much,' he said in a subdued tone. 'It's still a bit numb.'

'He was a good brave boy,' said Irene. 'We were very proud of him.' She added, 'I wondered if I ought to stay with her, but Simon wouldn't go without me, and Gladys had to come as I can't drive.'

Kym pulled her lips taut. 'She played the piano to amuse herself. She had plenty to think about!' And more, she thought ruefully, than you two imagine.

Mrs White placed a hand on Simon's shoulder. 'Why don't you run along upstairs, Simon, and play quietly for a while before dinner. We'll make you something nice you won't have to chew on too much.'

Simon sidled off, and Kai followed him, tail waving.

Mrs White smiled affectionately. 'He's a lovely little lad. He didn't make a fuss at all. Some kids yell blue murder.' She lowered her voice confidentially. 'It was a bit of a shock when she arrived. I thought she was still in America. Harley never said anything about her coming back early. I should have guessed I suppose. He hasn't had any trans-Atlantic telephone calls lately. She used to be very annoyed when she rang and he wasn't in.'

Irene put in, 'I suppose our being here has placed Harley in a bit of an awkward position.'

Kym smiled grimly. 'I imagine he will have a bit of

trouble explaining us to Lucinda. She's already jumped to a few wrong conclusions.'

'She gave me the impression she was practically engaged to him,' Irene admitted.

'That would appear to be the situation,' said Kym, and seeing her mother's downcast look, 'I did tell you, Mum . . .'

Mrs White suddenly chuckled. 'Do you know what she said, Kym? She said Harley had told her the decorators were in and the house was in too much of a mess to invite her round!'

'I know! She's livid about that deception, naturally. It's no wonder she suspected something in the end. It was a pretty thin excuse.'

'He could have asked us to go,' Irene said. 'We could have made other arrangements.'

'He wouldn't do that,' Mrs White said staunchly. 'Harley isn't the kind of man who breaks a promise, or changes his mind about doing a good deed.' She looked fondly at Kym. 'I really don't know what he sees in that . . . that flibbertigibbert. She's already made a mess of one marriage, and she's so snooty and selfish—well, I don't understand it at all. I just wish . . . I wish he'd come to his senses and marry a nice girl like you. He dotes on young Simon and the lad adores him like a father.'

Kym caught her breath. Surely Mrs White must have guessed the truth. But she gave no sign of it. Mrs White was very fond of Harley and believed he could do no wrong. She might be broadminded about his liking for female company, but she probably could never bring herself to believe he would get a girl into trouble. And that was probably why it had never crossed her mind that Simon could be Harley's son.

Kym said, 'But my father isn't Chairman of the hospital board and head of a prosperous pharmaceutical company.'

Mrs White drew herself up indignantly. 'I don't think Harley would marry her because of that!'

Kym had no intention of aggravating the housekeeper, so she dropped the subject, conceding, 'Maybe not . . .' and turned to her mother. 'You look a bit weary, Mum. Why don't you go up and have a rest for a while. I'll call you when dinner's ready.'

Irene agreed that she did feel a bit washed out, and so she left them to do as Kym had suggested.

Mrs White wiped her hands on her apron and opened the oven door to place a large casserole dish inside. She said to Kym, 'Would you mind doing the beans, dear? You'd better do a few extra since it looks as though we're going to have company for dinner.' She grimaced and Kym laughed.

Some little time later they heard Harley come in. Kym glanced at Mrs White and the housekeeper pursed her lips. They both paused, listening, but the only clue they got as to what was happening was that the piano had stopped.

Kym could not help wishing she could hear what was being said in the drawing room. Not that it would make much difference whether Lucinda believed Harley or not. She had made it quite clear that she wanted Harley, and nothing he did could change her mind about him. 'At least I won't have to feel responsible for breaking up their romance!' Kym thought.

Mrs White was just saying, 'I think we'll have to interrupt them, Kym. Dinner's nearly ready. Will you go or shall I?' when Harley appeared in the kitchen doorway.

'Lucinda won't be staying for dinner,' he informed them.

Kym was surprised, and searched his face for a clue as to why, but found nothing there. Possibly she would have felt embarrassed in view of her earlier conversation with Kym. She waited for him to say he wouldn't now be in for dinner either. But he said nothing.

Mrs White said, 'Oh dear, why not?'

'She seems to have remembered another engagement,' Harley answered.

And there the matter rested. He said nothing about Lucinda's visit at dinner, and Kym felt unable to broach the subject herself in front of the others, although there were a good many things she felt she wanted to say to him.

There was no opportunity afterwards, either, as immediately after dinner there was an urgent call from the hospital and he had to go out. Kym went to bed early, but she could not sleep. She kept puzzling over what might have happened between Harley and Lucinda. Had Lucinda in fact left in a huff? It seemed very likely, and yet she had appeared to Kym to be very forgiving of Harley. Kym's head swam with futile speculations as she stared at the bedroom ceiling, half hypnotised by the sweeping arcs of light across the darkness as cars turned into the square and their headlights beamed momentarily through her window. Each time she wondered if it was Harley returning.

She must have dozed off eventually because she was woken by a light tapping at her door and Harley's voice whispering urgently, 'Kym . . . are you awake?'

She glanced at the clock. It was just on midnight. 'What do you want?' she called in a whisper.

'Just a quick word.'

Kym struggled hurriedly into her dressing gown and opened the door. 'Can't it wait till morning?' she said.

'No!' He pushed her back into the room, and at the sight of her protesting eyes, laid a hand gently on her shoulder, saying, with a smile, 'It's all right, I promised . . .'

Her dubious gaze cut him off. 'Well, what is it?' she asked bluntly.

He looked at her for a long moment. 'I'm sorry you

had to cope with Lucinda this afternoon. I imagine she was in a pretty waspish mood.'

'She wasn't too happy at what she discovered,' admitted Kym. 'Having been told you had the decorators in!'

He chuckled unrepentantly.

'She jumped to all the wrong conclusions,' said Kym. 'I hope you set the record straight.'

His mouth quirked slightly. 'Oh, yes, I set the record straight.'

'She must have been pretty upset not to stay for dinner,' Kym said, 'or was she just embarrassed?'

He shrugged. 'Neither, I think. She just discovered a more pressing engagement, as I told you.'

Kym was cross. 'Harley, I know that isn't true! You've had a row, haven't you? Over us. Well, if it's any consolation, from what she said to me, she'll soon get over it. She's willing to forgive you practically anything.'

'Kym,' Harley said, in a firm tone, 'will you kindly stay out of my affairs? I am quite capable of managing Lucinda or anyone else. I just wanted to assure you that your being here is not an embarrassment, or an inconvenience, or any other sort of encumbrance Lucinda's visit might have suggested to you. You can forget about Lucinda.'

'Is she angry because you insist on seeing Simon after you're married?' Kym could not help asking, as the thought occurred to her.

'For heaven's sake, Kym!' he exclaimed, 'I don't want to discuss Lucinda, not now or any other time. I just want you to accept that there's no problem. I don't want you doing something silly and precipitate because she's been getting at you.'

'It might be better all round if we went back to the flat, though,' Kym said doubtfully. 'I told you Sue's sister . . .'

His hands dropped onto her shoulders. 'Damn Sue's sister! You're staying here until I say otherwise!'

She shrugged his hands away. 'There's no need to shout at me! You'll wake Simon.' She backed away from him angrily.

'I'm sorry.' He moved a step towards her, too suddenly for her to anticipate and move further away. His arms folded tightly around her and he held her hard against him and buried his face in her hair. He tilted her head back in a moment of savage passion and took her mouth in a violent kiss that made her senses swirl and her body reel. For an instant she was as transported as he was, then she pulled away.

'Harley, you promised . . .' she said almost on a sob.

His voice was husky. 'You can release me from that promise, Kym,' he whispered.

She shook her head. 'Harley, if it's so hard for you, I shouldn't be here. What is the matter with you? You've got Lucinda, you've got plenty of other women.'

He pulled her roughly back into his arms, crushing her cruelly against his hard muscular frame until she cried out. 'But none,' he said, his face very close to hers, 'that fire me as you do!'

'Go away,' she said bleakly. 'Please, just go away, and leave me alone.'

She closed her eyes, heard the door click shut, and he was gone. She crossed the room and flung herself on the bed, wishing she had never met Harley Garfield and fallen in love with him.

CHAPTER TEN

KYM felt as though she had done a hard day's work before she even began next day. She had been awake half the night deliberating on the impossible situation she was in, and she had made some very firm decisions. No more wavering and dithering, letting Harley dictate to her or letting her feelings for him lead her into foolish and pointless acts.

With the honesty that comes in the quiet hours of the night, she admitted to herself that she had let him take over when her mother was ill because deep down she wanted to be near him and could not bring herself to reject the opportunity. Perhaps she had even nurtured a lingering hope that he might fall in love with her. Desperately though she tried otherwise, her heart often ruled her head. It was high time she pulled herself together, she thought and started being one hundred per cent sensible and practical. As Harley was, she thought regretfully.

By morning it was all cut and dried in her mind. She and her mother and Simon would move back to the flat immediately, whatever Harley said. She would see Sue today and arrange to meet her sister. She crossed her fingers and hoped that Sue's sister would be willing to help out. As soon as she had organised it, she would tell her mother and Simon. And this time, she realised, there must be no procrastination. It was time to tell her mother the truth. It would be unfair to conceal it any longer, especially now that an outsider like Lucinda knew. Simon's reaction to having to go back to the flat she hardly dared contemplate, but resolved not to worry about that obstacle until the time came.

More terrifying was the opposition she expected from Harley.

But he must see how ridiculous the situation was. Why was he pig-headedly insisting on their staying, she puzzled, when it obviously was an inconvenience, whatever he said. And especially now that Lucinda had found out about it. The thought crossed her mind that perhaps he was using them to show Lucinda who was boss. She had undoubtedly demanded that they go, but Harley would not be dictated to, even by her, and he might keep them there at all costs in order to establish his authority. The more Kym thought about that the more she believed it might be true. Lucinda was a self-confident, independent young woman, an heiress, accustomed to having her own way, too. But Harley would not want to be ruled by his wife.

'I'm sure that's it . . .' Kym said to herself, convinced. 'He's just using us as pawns to suit his game with her. Well, we're not going to be that!' She clenched her teeth determinedly. If Lucinda interpreted their leaving Lowther Square as a victory, it was too bad. Harley would have to find some other way to bring her to heel.

'I'm getting bitter,' Kym said to her reflection as she was making up her face. 'And cynical.'

It was raining when she left the house. Harley was not driving her today. She sloshed along to the tube station on leaden feet, wishing that it could all be accomplished with the speed it took to think of it. But, it was, after all, her own fault she was in this mess. She should never have allowed it to happen.

The day began badly. Everything seemed to conspire to depress her spirits, and hinder her plans. When she arrived early on Pepys ward, Sister beamed at her.

'Oh, good, you're nice and early, Nurse Rutherford. I hope you're feeling fit and energetic!'

'Why's that?' Kym asked.

'They're short-staffed on Wren again, and you're to

transfer there for the time being. You've been on Wren before, haven't you?'

Kym nodded. Today of all days she didn't want to go back there. They didn't see much of Harley on Pepys where she had been for a few days. But she had no option.

'Better go down there straight away,' said the senior nurse. 'We can manage all right here.'

There was one good thing about it, Kym thought to herself as she hurried along the corridor to Wren, she might have an earlier chance of talking to Sue, and if she could find a moment to contact her sister . . . Her mind was racing ahead. She might even manage to get the whole thing settled tonight.

When she walked into Wren she ought to have known it was a bad omen that it was Sister Fremlin's shift, not the pleasanter and easier to work for, Sister Muir.

'Good morning, Sister,' Kym said. 'I was told to report to Wren this morning. I believe you're short-staffed.'

Sister Fremlin looked her over briefly. She had always regarded Kym with an air of disapproval, probably, Kym thought, because she had given up nursing for so long, and worked in an office. Sister Fremlin believed nursing was a vocation, and that anyone who gave it up for reasons other than raising a family, was suspect.

'Nurse Grant is away ill,' said Sister through tight lips. In her book only patients were ever ill. 'And we're one short on the next shift as well.'

Kym's heart was sinking. Sue away ill. That was a blow. It meant she was not going to be able to talk to her today after all. And she might also have to do some extra duty.

'What's wrong with Nurse Grant?' she asked.

'Influenza apparently,' sniffed Sister Fremlin. 'I suppose she hasn't had her jabs.'

'I don't think anyone has yet, have they?' Kym said. She had not heard about it, but as a rule influenza vaccinations were provided for all the staff before winter set in. 'It's a bit early.'

'It seems it's never too early for influenza,' said Sister frostily. 'She should have had some protection if she had an inoculation last year.'

Kym knew the perils of arguing with Sister Fremlin, but she couldn't help saying, 'Vaccination is not always complete protection, if there's a new strain about, and I know people who manage to get the flu whether they have their jabs or not.'

Sister Fremlin stared at her over her spectacles. 'Quite so,' she said briskly, 'but standing here discussing it is not getting the work done. Dr Garfield will be round this morning, and we have a lot to do. The first thing you had better do is turn Mr Phillips. Get Nurse James to help you, and then . . .'

Kym, with great difficulty in concentration, listened to the list of special tasks required of her, as well as the routine special feeding of two patients, temperature and blood-pressure readings, bed making and tidying duties that were a part of every day's nursing. All she wanted to think about today was that Sue was sick, and her plan for immediate action ruined. And to make it worse, it was Harley's day for visiting the ward. She felt quite sick herself.

She also felt quite stupidly self-conscious when Harley came into the ward with a registrar and a houseman, and she was relieved that Sister Fremlin did not ask her to accompany them. She continued doing her tasks as though he were just any consultant and of no particular interest to her at all. Once or twice she caught his eye and he flashed her a swift, clandestine smile, and her heart turned over as involuntary colour flooded her cheeks. He paused only once as she was passing and spoke to her directly.

'So you're back on Wren for a while, Nurse Rutherford?'

'Yes, sir,' she answered impersonally.

'We're very short-staffed here at the moment,' Sister Fremlin put in. 'With two nurses off sick.'

Harley smiled sympathetically. 'There seems to be a nasty flu virus going around. A lot of people have it. A sort of late summer survivor!'

Sister Fremlin did not smile. 'I only hope nobody else goes down with it,' she said, looking accusingly at Kym as though she thought she might do so deliberately.

Kym, who already felt worse than any flu germ could make her, said, 'I hope not,' and moved on.

A short time later when Sister Fremlin had gone for her lunch break, Kym took the opportunity to use the typewriter in Sister's office to type a letter. It was her letter of resignation, and she found it extremely difficult to write. She screwed up several attempts and was half way through a new one when Harley appeared in the doorway.

'What's the trouble?' he asked, coming in and perching on the edge of the desk. He had an envelope of X-rays in his hand.

'Trouble?'

'You looked positively thunderous as I came in. What are you trying to do?' He leaned forward, peering over the typewriter to see what she was typing, and Kym was not swift enough in tearing the sheet out of the machine to prevent him seeing it.

He came round beside her and wrested the now crumpled paper from her fingers. 'What's this? Your resignation!'

Kym thought bleakly, it never goes the way I plan when he's involved. The first day I came here I messed it all up, and now it's all going wrong again. She felt close to tears.

His face was too close to hers for comfort, and the

grey-blue eyes were searching her face. 'Why are you resigning?'

There was no point in prevaricating. She had meant to confront him with a *fait accompli*, but fate had seen fit to foil her plans, so she decided she might as well tell him now what she intended and that she was not going to stand for any interference from him this time.

She took a deep breath. 'Harley . . . for all our sakes, I've decided I must leave St Alphage's right away, and I am arranging to move out of your house immediately, too. Now that Mum is almost fit again, there is no real reason why we should stay.'

'Is this because of last night?' he asked, his face expressionless.

'No . . . well, yes, partly . . . That and other things.' She could not tell him that she believed he might be using her in his battle with Lucinda. 'The plain fact is, I believe it will be better for both of us if I do not work at St A's. You are, of course, at liberty to see Simon any time you wish.'

'Thank you,' he said, and standing back from her, regarded her contemplatively. He went on, 'I suppose you're right.' He smiled regretfully. 'You were perfectly justified when you said I had no right to ride roughshod over you. I haven't. Perhaps I was a little too impetuous, too hasty, and too sure of myself. I met my match in you, Kym.'

Kym's mouth almost fell open in astonishment. This was not the reaction she had expected at all, and she was almost disappointed, having geared herself to fight him yet again. But of course it couldn't go on like that. He knew it as well as she did. Now Lucinda was back in the picture he was regretting his rash behaviour. He could blame it all on the shock of discovering he had a son. It didn't matter. What mattered now was that everything must quickly return to normal. There could never be complete normality again, Kym knew, because the fact of Harley knowing about Simon could not be erased. They would all have to adapt a little to accommodate that new situation.

'Which was just as well in the circumstances,' she said. What would he be thinking now, she wondered, if she had agreed to marry him the first time he had asked? Would he be trying to get out of it? Or would he go through with it, thus condemning them both to a life of resentment and bitterness?

He handed her the crumpled sheet of paper. She would have had to start it again anyway.

'When do you plan to move?' he asked without expression.

This new acquiescent Harley made Kym feel uneasy. It crossed her mind that perhaps he had come to see her at this time, hoping Sister Fremlin would be out of the way. Doubtless he had been thinking things ever since last night too. Perhaps he had been going to suggest precisely the same solution she had. She had beaten him to it, and she was glad of that.

'I thought the weekend,' Kym said. 'If that's all right with you.' It was only two days away.

'What arrangements are you making about Simon?' For the first time his face showed a flicker of anxiety.

'Remember, I told you about Sue Grant's sister . . . ?' Kym said. 'I think she'll be able to help me out. Sue's away ill at the moment so I haven't been able to ask her about it yet.' She added, 'Sue's sister is a nurse, too, so she'll keep an eye on Mum for me.'

Harley turned away briefly, and seemed almost to be talking to himself as he murmured, 'Maybe I should have let you do that in the first place.'

'Well, you weren't to know Lucinda would come back earlier than expected,' Kym pointed out. She added, 'You should have told me she was back and we'd have made other arrangements.'

He whipped around and his face was angry, his eyes

blazing. He seemed about to rail at her, then he abruptly turned away again, shrugging his shoulders. Kym thought she heard him mutter, 'Oh, what's the use!'

'I really am very grateful to you, Harley,' Kym said sincerely. 'I know you meant well, and you did try to make things turn out for the best for everybody, but . . . well, it's just one of those things, I suppose. We can't call back the past and alter it.' For a moment she felt too choked to go on, then she managed to say, 'You . . . you will want to go on seeing Simon?'

He fixed her with his steely gaze for a long long moment, and finally he said very slowly as though it gave him considerable pain, 'I don't know. Perhaps it might be better for all concerned if I didn't.'

Kym drew a sharp breath. Did this mean that Lucinda had issued an ultimatum? It certainly looked like it. Harley's very subdued manner this morning, his lack of opposition to her plans, and suggesting it might be better not to see Simon, indicated that Lucinda had won. Last night he had been willing to fight her, but reflecting on it, he had doubtless decided that he wanted what Lucinda had to offer more than he wanted his son. He was going to give in. If only she could despise him for that, Kym thought suddenly, she would be half way cured . . .

She said quietly, 'Well, of course that's up to you. If you prefer not to, I quite understand. Simon will be very upset at first, naturally . . .'

'He'll soon forget,' Harley said, and she could see that the decision had not been made lightly. His feelings for the boy, if nothing else, were genuine, and Kym felt the pain she knew this wrench was causing him. She blamed herself. She should never have let him discover he had a son. Harley added harshly, 'Especially if you marry— Masters or anyone else.'

Kym did not answer that, and a moment or two later he went on in a matter-of-fact tone, 'I shall set up a trust for him, with you to have discretionary use of the income. You can let me know how he is progressing from time to time.'

Kym suddenly felt close to tears in the long, highly charged silence that followed. She might have completely lost her fragile composure if one of the junior nurses had not come to the office door and tapped lightly on the glass before opening it and looking hesitantly in.

'Nurse Rutherford . . . .' the girl said, a worried frown on her face.

Kym snapped out of her dismal reverie, and Harley too seemed to crash back to earth from somewhere remote. He glanced at the nurse hovering in the doorway, and said crisply to Kym, 'I'll leave the plates with you, Nurse. I'll talk to Sister about the patient another time.' He picked up the envelope he had earlier placed on the desk, put it down again, and walked out of the office.

Kym dealt with the minor query raised by the other nurse, who was new on the ward, regarding whether Mr Grainger should or should not be allowed to get up and sit for an hour or two in the day room watching television. He had insisted that he was allowed to do so. Kym consulted the patient's file.

'There's nothing in his notes about it and Sister didn't mention it to me,' Kym said, 'so we'd better wait until she gets back. She should be here any minute. You go off to lunch and I'll deal with it.'

Kym didn't bother to go to lunch that day. She did not feel hungry and she did not feel in the mood for frivolous gossip, or the usual complaints and criticisms that often permeated nurses' conversations. Neither did she feel in the mood to hear about their romances.

She brooded deeply over Harley's complete change of attitude, glad that she had taken the plunge and said her piece. It looked as though things were going to revert to the way they had been before. And that was, as Harley had said, probably all for the best. She would leave St Alphage's, find work somewhere else—perhaps they would even leave London . . . She latched on to that thought with some eagerness. Perhaps they could go somewhere in the country and she could get a house with a garden for Simon, and work in the local hospital, or even as a district nurse. Her mother had always said she liked the country. She would talk to her about it. These burgeoning new ideas helped to take some of the edge off her real feelings, but she knew that because of what she had done and what had happened, her love for Harley had strengthened, and because of that she would always regret that Simon had been deprived of his real father.

It was a hectic day on the ward, and by the end of her shift, Kym was feeling rather weary, drained physically and emotionally. She longed to relax in a warm bath and go to bed, but knew she could not properly enjoy it or relax in Harley's house. She could not be gone from there soon enough now she knew it was what he wanted too. Tonight she would tell her mother, she resolved, and that was an ordeal she did not look forward to. Irene would take it in her stride as she took most things, but Kym did not relish now any more than she had before, telling her mother the truth.

She was a little late changing over at the end of her shift as there were more instructions than usual to be passed on, and notes to be written up. She was still in the ward when Harley suddenly appeared. He was in street clothes and had obviously been out because his hair glistened with raindrops. Kym had been too busy to notice that it was raining again. She wondered why he had come back, and to see her.

He had a grim expression, and Kym suddenly tensed as panic rose in her swiftly. 'Is something wrong?' Her thoughts flew to Simon . . . her mother . . .

'I was afraid you might already have left,' he said,

sounding breathless, as from hurrying. 'Have you nearly finished?'

She nodded. 'Yes, but . . .'

'I'll be waiting in the car park,' he rapped out, and there was a gravelly edge to his voice, almost as though he was suppressing anger. It was a command he expected to be obeyed and he did not wait for an answer. Sister Fremlin came to the door of her office just as Harley thrust his broad frame outwards through the ward doors. She was obviously annoyed that he had spoken to a nurse and not to her. 'What did Dr Garfield want?' she demanded, tight-lipped.

Kym stared blankly at her, still taken aback by Harley's abrupt arrival and departure and peremptory command. 'Oh just something about my mother . . .' It was the first thing that came into her head.

Sister Fremlin sniffed, but as it was personal and in the province of a consultant, she forebore to enquire further. She said starchily, 'If you've finished, Nurse, you might as well go now.'

'Yes, Sister, thank you.' Kym fled, swiftly changing out of her uniform into blouse and skirt and raincoat, and tying a scarf around her hair. She felt apprehensive as she sped down to the hospital car park. He had looked very peculiar. She had never seen him in such a grim mood before and she was perplexed.

He held the passenger door open for her, slammed it behind her and without uttering a word slid behind the driving wheel.

'Harley, what's wrong?' she demanded.

'Nothing,' he replied tersely.

'There must be,' she insisted. 'What's the matter?'

He remained stubbornly silent as he swung the big car out of the car park into the road, and paused briefly at the nearby traffic lights. Still he said nothing, and Kym kept silent, knowing that to persist might only aggravate him more and cause him to drive erratically. He would, presumably, tell her what was on his mind, when he was ready.

She stared ahead through the windscreen, half-hypnotised by the windscreen-wipers' monotonous whirring and only half-seeing the passing scene. She was unaware of the direction they were travelling in, assuming it was to Lowther Square, until some building or landmark they passed struck a discordant note in her brain and jerked her into awareness.

'Harley, this isn't the way home. Where are we going?'

He glanced at her, and for the first time a faint smile curved his lips. 'Just for a drive,' he said infuriatingly.

'What for?' Kym felt irritated. What was he up to now? She had planned her evening precisely, and he was threatening to upset her plans with this peculiar behaviour.

He did not answer. Kym persisted, 'Harley, what is this? Where are you taking me? We're late . . . Mrs White will have dinner ready.'

'I told her we might be late. We're going to a nice quiet place where we can talk.'

Kym slumped back. 'What about?'

'Us.'

'But we've been through all that . . .' What on earth could he mean, she wondered, uneasily. What kind of crazy proposal was he going to come up with now?

They continued in silence for some time until Kym became aware that they were heading towards Richmond. Not until they were in a remote part of the park did Harley stop the car. There was no-one about and it was getting dark. Kym felt suddenly very apprehensive.

'What's this in aid of?' she asked nervously.

He turned to look fully at her, but his face, although close to her, was in shadow and she could not see the expression in his eyes. She could feel the tension crackling between them, however, and the slight but visible twitch at the corner of his mouth betrayed an uncharacteristic nervousness in him too. She had the feeling that he was holding something back with effort.

He rasped tersely, 'It isn't rape if that's what you're worried about. I just want to talk to you without the slightest fear of anyone interrupting. No phones, no people, nothing.'

'Well, you picked the right place,' she said, attempting to contrast his tone with lightness, and a nervous smile. 'But I wish you'd tell me what this is all about.'

'There is something we have to get straightened out. No evasions, no prevarications, just the truth.'

'I really don't know what you're getting at.'

He waited a moment, leaning back against the car door so that he was still looking at her, his arm laid along the back of the seat, his fingers drumming lightly on the soft leather covers. Kym licked dry lips and waited, knowing he was purposely goading her, whipping her into a ferment of frustration, as some kind of punishment. For what? They had settled everything today, hadn't they?

Rain drummed on the car roof and streamed off the windows.

At last he spoke, in a carefully controlled voice. 'I left the hospital at lunch time today. I went home. I was feeling very depressed. Your mother was in the house alone, Mrs White having gone out shopping. We had a long talk . . .' He paused.

'So?' Kym queried, mystified.

'It was just about this and that, and then we got around to rather personal matters.'

Kym was growing impatient now, and a little annoyed with him. 'Harley, I give up. What on earth did she say to make you rush me off into the middle of Richmond Park in the pouring rain?'

'She doesn't know that I am Simon's father.'

'No,' Kym agreed, unable to see what his point could

be, 'and you know that she doesn't know. However, I intend to tell her when we get home. I think it's time she heard the whole story. I've been a bit of a coward about it, but for a long time I didn't want anyone—least of all you—to know.'

He did not seem to be listening to her. 'Irene is very anxious about you and your future,' Harley said, 'and she confessed as much to me. Quite naturally she jumped to rather hasty conclusions about my interest in you.'

'I told her all along that you were going to marry Lucinda,' Kym said, still not sure where all this was leading.

He thumped the back of the seat. 'Lucinda! Lucinda! You have Lucinda on the brain. I am not going to marry Lucinda!'

Kym's eyes widened in astonishment. She must have been wrong after all, concluding that Lucinda had won. What could have happened? Lucinda had seemed so ready to forgive, and then Harley so willing to give in. She said soberly, 'And it's all our fault . . . oh, Harley, I am sorry, but you did rather bring it on yourself, deceiving her . . .'

'Do be quiet, Kym,' he said sharply, 'It is not your fault. I never had any intention of marrying Lucinda.'

'But she said . . . everyone thought . . .' Kym was aghast.

He laughed harshly. 'Oh, yes, you've all been very busy behind my back organising my life for me, haven't you? Pushing me into Lucinda's arms.' He shuddered. 'Lucinda isn't my kind of woman!'

Kym said defensively, 'You were seen out with her a lot, dancing cheek to cheek, holding hands over champagne . . . and obviously she would be very good for your career. Most people think it was Lucinda's influence that got you the consultant's job.'

'The devil they do!' he exclaimed, showing some

annoyance. He went on derisively, 'The hospital grapevine is obviously very efficient!' A mischievous glint came into his eyes. 'Perhaps I did lead her on a bit. She asked for it!'

'Harley, you're pretending you don't care. She has turned you down after all, hasn't she? She's furious with you for being, as she sees it, unfaithful.'

'You astound me,' he said with sarcasm. 'You know so much!'

Kym offered consolation. 'Look, you probably don't need to worry too much. Give her time. She's probably just punishing you. She'll make you sweat for a while, then she'll come round. When she spoke to me she was willing enough to forgive you anything, at least that was my impression.'

He leaned forward slightly, until his hand closed over her shoulder. 'Kym, Lucinda was never in the position of needing to dispense forgiveness. She went too far yesterday. I decided I had put up with her unwelcome advances long enough, and to hell with my promise to her father.'

'Your . . . promise?' echoed Kym, mystified.

'Your grapevine didn't get it quite right,' he said grimly. 'My interest in Lucinda was because her father begged me to take her in hand and knock some sense into her. We happen to be friends, Charles Raymond and I. He was pretty cut up when she got divorced. He hadn't approved of her marrying in the first place. He said he didn't want her going through unsuitable husbands on a whim, like she went through clothes. He wanted her to settle down and produce heirs to his empire!'

'And he thought you were an ideal candidate to father them?' Kym suggested.

Harley shook his head. 'Not at all. I'm afraid Charles, friend though he is, wants something better for his daughter than a mere consultant physician, but he believed I could be a temporary steadying influence. He didn't expect Lucinda to consider marrying me!'

Kym could not help a burst of laughter.

He said in hurt tones, 'Not everyone sees me the way you do!'

'I'm sorry.'

'Then he rather suddenly packed her off to friends in America, and turned a bit cool on me—I suspect because she was silly enough to tell him she wanted to marry me.'

'You said yourself you encouraged her,' said Kym.

'Not to that extent! I made it quite clear all along I wasn't interested in marriage. You won't believe this, I suppose, but Lucinda didn't appeal to me in any other way, either. I realise now that this only made her more determined to have me. I squired her around wherever she wanted to go, talked to her like a Dutch uncle and tried to persuade her into doing something useful with her life instead of simply husband-hunting, but I failed. When that girl makes up her mind, it's the devil's own job to change it. She came back from the States and told her father she intended to marry me whether he liked it or not. She then proceeded to hound me.' He paused, then went on in a different tone, laced with some asperity, 'As for whether I got my job through her, that's a load of nonsense. I didn't get it because Charles is a friend, either. I got where I am by earning it! With years of hard work and study.'

Kym said softly, 'You can't deny, Harley, that you gave the impression you were going to marry Lucinda— you did to me at any rate.'

A faint smile lifted one corner of his mouth. 'There's a crazy perversity in me sometimes. It leads me to do and say things on the spur of the moment . . .'

'Harley,' persisted Kym, 'why else would you have kept Lucinda away from Lowther Square, telling her the decorators were in? You didn't want her to know we were living there. You knew how she would view it.'

His fingers tightened hurtfully on her shoulder. 'You
bet I knew how she would see it, and I didn't want the
whole hospital buzzing with the news until . . .' He
stopped abruptly, smiling enigmatically at her. 'Well,
we'll come to that in a minute.'

'What on earth do you mean?'

He did not answer her question, but after a moment's
silence, he went on, 'I rather let my hair down this
afternoon, talking to your mother.' He chuckled. 'It's a
wonder you didn't feel your ears burning.'

'I can't imagine what you found to discuss about me,'
Kym said, slightly nettled. They seemed to getting no-
where so far as she could see. She felt a strange kind of
relief that he was not going to marry Lucinda, and was
paradoxically glad that he was still the free spirit she had
always believed him to be, who didn't want to be tied
down to anyone, but that didn't make any difference,
alas, to their relationship.

Harley said slowly, 'I told your mother that I was
concerned about you, about what you might be contem-
plating doing. I asked her what she thought about Joel
Masters as a son-in-law.'

Kym said hotly, 'You had no right . . .'

'No. But I can't seem to help interfering in your life,
can I?'

'What did she say?' Kym knew without having to ask.

'She told me you were not seeing him any more, that
you hadn't been out with him for some time.' He held
her gaze, demanding the truth. 'Is that true, Kym?'

'Ye . . . es,' she admitted reluctantly.

Still his eyes bored into hers. 'I said to your mother
that maybe you weren't seeing him, but you were probably still in love with him.'

Kym averted her eyes and did not speak.

'Your mother said she was sure you weren't in love
with Joel. She said she had almost despaired of your ever

falling in love with another man because you had never taken any man seriously since . . . what she said was that she was sure you were still in love with someone in the past, and that instead of time being the cure, it only seemed to make things worse because since you'd returned to England you'd become very morose.'

'Don't . . .' Kym gasped involuntarily.

'When I asked if she meant the Australian you had married, at first she said yes, she believed so, and then she changed her mind and told me the truth, the truth I already knew of course, that you never were married, but also the truth I didn't know—that the man you were eating your heart out over, the only man you had ever loved, was *Simon's father* . . .'

Kym could only look fixedly into her lap, her brain seemed to have gone numb. So now he knew.

He went on relentlessly, 'She told me that in her opinion only being swept off your feet by someone else would cure you, and that she'd been hoping I'd be the one to do it. Dear Irene! She actually likes me, even though you insisted I was going to marry Lucinda.' He paused, drawing a deep breath before going on, 'I explained about Lucinda, and she was astonished. Then she admitted that she'd always felt sure I must be in love with you.'

Kym covered her face with her hands. 'How . . . how embarrassing for you.'

His hand slid from her shoulder and touched her fingers, and then both his hands were prising hers from her stricken face. He held them tightly clasped inside his large palms. 'I told your mother, Kym, that I had always loved you, and for much longer than she imagined.'

Kym opened her eyes. She stared into his face, disbelieving.

He was smiling at her. 'She didn't quite understand, of course, so I didn't tell her everything—that is your prerogative anyway—but she said it was a pity you didn't love me, that you were wasting your life carrying a torch for this—as she put it—phantom lover!'

Kym swallowed hard, and it was a moment or two before she found her voice. 'Harley . . . what exactly are you saying?'

'I'm saying I love you.' He raised her hands to his lips. 'I always have.'

'But you can't have . . . you never told me you did . . .'

'I told you that night we made love . . .'

'And regretted it next morning,' she said bitterly. 'You were at pains to emphasise that your career was more important to you than marriage. You implied that just because we'd slept together I needn't read anything into it.'

He held her hands against his heart. 'And don't I regret that now! It was only half true. But you had said similar things. Neither of us really wanted to be tied down then. I didn't *want* to love you because I thought it would upset my plans. I didn't think you cared for me very much—you had other boyfriends. I was just one of them. You never gave any sign you thought me special. You gave me a very firm brush-off in fact.'

Kym sighed. 'I didn't want to love you either. I didn't want to be hurt. I thought you might want to have an affair, and I didn't want that.'

'So when you discovered you were pregnant you ran away rather than risk marriage to a man you thought didn't love you?'

'I didn't know you would marry me . . .'

'Oh, Kym,' he said softly, 'If we'd only been more honest!'

She shook her head. 'It wasn't a question of honesty. I knew I couldn't marry you, even if you wanted to, if you didn't love me, because I feared that one day you might meet someone you did.'

'You could have asked me,' he said quietly.

'I guess I was too proud to discuss such deep feelings. I was very mixed up, Harley. I didn't want to hear you say no. I didn't want to be humiliated, the lovesick little nurse, in trouble, trying to catch her man by getting pregnant . . .'

He pulled her hard against him. 'Oh, my poor little Kym. What you must have been through.'

She looked up at him. 'It wasn't all bad.' She smiled bravely. Then she said, 'But if you . . . if you really did . . . do love me . . . why didn't you say so when you asked me to marry you. You knew I wouldn't marry without love.'

'Without *your* love, I thought you meant. I confess I thought that if you had loved me you could have said yes, but you didn't, so . . . well, now I know I was wrong. And seven years ago I was, like you, reluctant to admit I was in love. Out of pride, too, I suppose. And when you came back I was afraid that if you knew it, you might retreat even further from me. I soon discovered you were still attracted to me, I hoped you might fall in love with me.'

'But you asked me to marry you, believing I was not,' she said, not fully comprehending.

'Discovering Simon was my son did rather complicate matters,' he said, half apologetically. 'I acted hastily. I was afraid of losing you to someone else, and I foolishly thought you would marry me for Simon's sake, and the rest would come later. When you refused I still arrogantly believed I could make you love me. If only I'd realised that you already did, we could have saved ourselves a great deal of heartache.'

Kym studied his face intently. 'Harley, you don't have to pretend you've loved me all the time, just because you found out that I . . .'

'I'm not pretending, love. It's true. When you disappeared from St A's, and out of my life, I realised suddenly what I'd lost. All I knew then was that you'd ditched me, and then gone off to Australia pursuing a career, a love of travel and adventure. I tried to forget you and that one night we spent together, but it was indelibly imprinted on my mind. I went around with other girls, but for a long time it was your face that haunted me, you I fancied I held in my arms. I never thought I'd see you again, and finally the time came when I thought that at last I had got you out of my system.

'And then, out of the blue, you collapsed at my feet in the corridor of the hospital. I was never so profoundly shocked in all my life. I thought I'd conquered your ghost and there, suddenly, it was all flooding back, choking me. And as if that wasn't enough, though I had remained faithful, in spirit, for years, you had apparently heartlessly fallen in love with some rough, tough Australian and married him! And had a child.

'I felt cheated, humiliated and I hated you! But I couldn't keep it up for long. The old magic was still there, and I was sure you felt it too, so I set out to win you back. Then what did I discover? That Simon is my son . . . mine! That your child is *our* love-child and there never was a husband. I was shattered when you stubbornly refused to marry me. It had to be because you were in love with someone else, and naturally I thought it was Joel. I never dreamed it was me! Why should I? You let me think our love-making had been only a casual encounter to you, a silly prank on the night of the Nurses' Ball. It was just bad luck that you'd become pregnant. You can't imagine how jealous I was of Joel, Kym. I am very angry with you for deceiving me!'

'Harley, I'm sorry . . .' It was all she could say.

He went on, 'All those years, Kym, I swear there was never anyone I wanted to marry. Can you imagine how I felt when I discovered Simon was my son—by the girl I was in love with, but who I knew didn't love me? I was frantic. I had to find a way out of the dilemma. I behaved like a clumsy fool. I used the strong physical attraction between us, which you couldn't deny, to try and take you away from Joel. But you resisted my every effort. I thought having you under my roof might make you see me differently, but no, you still seemed stuck on him!'

'You let me think you were going to marry Lucinda. You never denied it,' she countered.

He smirked. 'I was only trying to make you jealous!'

'You certainly did that,' Kym said.

He drew her towards him and clasped his arms tightly around her again. 'If only I'd realised it. You were so good at keeping your true feelings to yourself. Tell me, Kym—say it—is it true that you love me?'

She held him closer still. 'It's true. I couldn't get you out of my mind, ever, and these past months have been hell, the worst time of my life, because I had you and yet didn't have you. I thought it was only Simon you wanted, and I was torn between believing I ought to marry you for Simon's sake, or refusing for my own. I thought you wanted to marry Lucinda, but were willing to make a sacrifice for Simon, but I couldn't bring myself to make a similar sacrifice, it would have hurt too much. I knew I couldn't bear seeing you leave me for another woman's arms whenever you felt like it. You even suggested we could get divorced later if we wanted to.'

'To give you a let-out. Anything to make you say yes!' He chuckled. 'I would never have let you divorce me!'

'You can't imagine the torment it's been, living a lie,' Kym said, relaxing against his shoulder, her head buried against his neck.

'I can, my love. I've suffered too. Having you in my house was the last straw. One minute it was exquisite joy, being a family in fact if not in name, the next bleak despair because I knew it couldn't go on like that forever. When I'd pass your door at night, the urge to rush in and take you in my arms was sometimes more than I could bear.'

'I thought desire was all you felt for me,' Kym whispered.

'I told you, you know so little about me.'

He bent his head and kissed her tenderly. There was no savage passion now, no urgent desire, only a gentle seeking and discovery. Kym felt a great wave of happiness wash over her.

'I had to make up my mind to go,' she said a few moments later. 'I couldn't stand it any longer. After you came to my room last night . . . it was too much.'

He stroked her cheek. 'I felt the same. I thought I'd lost the battle completely. I realised it was useless trying to coerce you, that you would never love me, and you would probably marry that crass houseman! I don't accept defeat lightly, but I decided it would be better if we didn't see each other again, and that meant not seeing Simon either. It was a terrible decision to have to make, but I resolved I wouldn't try to see him again after you all left. I couldn't see him without seeing you, and seeing you without having you was likely to drive me insane.'

'I thought your decision was because of Lucinda,' Kym said. 'I know she wouldn't want you to visit us. I thought she must have delivered an ultimatum, her or Simon.'

He tilted her chin and looked into her eyes. 'My God, what an imagination! You ought to write books!'

They both laughed, rocking helplessly in each other's arms as though it was a hilarious joke, but the laughter was not at a silly remark, it was the release of pent-up emotion and almost unbearable tension that both had endured for so long.

'Well, what did happen?' Kym asked, as the paroxysm subsided.

He grinned. 'I stuck my neck right out—I told her I was going to marry *you*!'

'But you thought . . . you didn't know . . .'

He looked sheepish. 'I know, but I had to stop her nonsense somehow, and there didn't seem to be another way. I knew she wouldn't gossip about it. Her pride wouldn't let her!'

'Oh, Harley!' was all Kym could say. Then she added tentatively, 'What about Simon? Are we going to tell him you're his father?'

He brushed a strand of hair from her forehead, began to tuck it under the scarf that was still knotted around her head, then pushed the square of thin silk off her hair and ran his fingers through the thick dark curls in a movement that was all at once electrifying. Kym felt the stirrings of desire in him as well as deep within herself, and waited impatiently for his kiss.

He answered her question first. 'Not yet, I think,' he said in soft husky tones. 'Let's get married first—all the trimmings, very proper—and he can go on calling me "uncle" for a while until he's a bit too old to do that any more, and by then the time might be ripe for him to know the truth. And by then also, I expect other people will have forgotten just how long we've been married!'

Kym breathed happily, 'Who cares if they haven't! So long as we are together, what else matters?'

The rain drummed relentlessly down on the roof of the car, and streamed off the windows. It was quite impossible to drive home yet.

Harley said gently, 'Exactly, my own sweet love. What else matters?'